PRINTHOUSE BOOKS PRESENTS

I0561648

Hispanicus
The Apostate Life of Antonio Pintero

Eddie Cisneros
Crime Drama

PrintHouse Books, Atlanta, GA.

Published: 8-1-2017

www.PrintHouseBooks.com

VIP INK Publishing Group; Incorporated

Cover art designed by SK7.
Editor: Shelby Oates

ISBN: 978-1-5323-4886-0

Library of Congress Cataloging-in-Publication Data
LCCN #2017948738

1. Urban Literature 2. True Fiction
2. Crime 4.Eddie Cisneros 5.SouthBronx, N.Y.

Printed in the United States of America

To my family: Thanks for the love and support.
To my friends: Thanks for keeping it 100% real.

"Writing a story may take several years, whereas, actually reading it may take a few hours. But as long as I can continue to captivate readers I will continue writing."

PRINTHOUSE BOOKS
Read it, Enjoy it, Tell a friend.
VIP INK Publishing Group, Incorporated.
Atlanta, GA
www.PrintHouseBooks.com

Table of Contents

Foreword:

Hispanicus

The Apostate Life of Antonio Pintero

"I've lived the life of a rock star! I had everything and anything you could possibly think of, I had it all: the money, women, cars, clothes, and jewelry. People often say when you live fast, you die young. Shit, if that's the case then my life was that of a slick, motherfucking turbo charged Lamborghini, racing at ultimate speeds, so the problem with that logic is — I'm still alive. Truth is, I shouldn't be though."

··········

I just laid there on the bed, with a pained look on my face, hands behind my head. The cheap motel we were in had an added touch of vanity as I stared up at the mirrors on the ceiling looking at my pathetic self.

Having once lived a glorified life, things were a lot different now. Then my eyes got watery. I'd finally experienced an epiphany of sorts, but deep down inside I knew I would never be able to change the actions I had taken upon myself and others. I knew it was all catching up to me, and fast. I laid there, wallowing in my own misery, all the while some cheap crackhead hooker furiously attempted to suck on my limp cock. She finally gave up and got off the bed.

"This is fucking useless!" She said dejectedly, as she gave me a nasty look to boot. She then proceeded to walk into the bathroom, possibly to try and Listerine the failed blow-job for quick cash off her breath.

That was the beginning of the end.

Chapter 1

"Growing Up is Hard to Do"

Allow me to get the formalities out of the way. My name is Antonio Pintero, and I was born in 1976. My mother's name was Mildred Cepeda. She was a heroin addict and died of AIDS when I was fourteen-years-old. I never knew my father. He was probably some random guy she thought she was in love with, at whatever time in her life he happened to show up. He injected her with his share of the Y chromosome, produced me, and then split. You know how that goes. *Mother: baby. Father: maybe?*

I became a statistic for the system, stamped with a question mark on my forehead regarding dear old daddy. *Fuck him!* Whoever he was.

After the sperm donor dipped, my mother then met Rolando Pintero. He was one of those Cuban exiles who hopped aboard a boat at Mariel Harbor, and made his way to Miami. Rolando was considered the cream of the crop. Once in Miami, he and a few relatives journeyed to New York. He spent much of his life either locked up in jail or in mental institutions for being a borderline psychotic.

I also have a younger brother, Miguel. He was the product of a cursed inception by two people who should have never even had children. Miguel was born mentally retarded — Oh, excuse me, "developmentally disabled." I disconnected with Miguel for a very long time, until years later, when I finally grew enough balls to track him down. As for me? Well, I'll start off like this: It was 1981, and I was five years old.

....

Rolando entered the kitchen area with a black backpack in hand. He cleared the table off and emptied the contents of the pack. There was the "business stuff", a collective made of three ounces of marijuana, a zip lock bag filled with a hundred packets of heroin, it seemed, and some odd colored pills in another bag; a carton of Viceroy cigarettes for his personal use lay right on top.

Rolando was in his late thirties. He stood about six feet, his right foot aided by a shoe lift to balance everything out due to a length discrepancy. He could easily capture anyone's attention in a room because of his gait, but no one ever dared to make fun of him. He was always about business before pleasure; therefore, he carried a scowl on his face regularly.

"Mildred!" he screamed, as he opened his carton of cigs.

He pulled the pack out and vigorously tapped on the bottom, making sure the tobacco would be nicely packed.

"Mildred, what the fuck?" he screamed again. Rolando opened the pack, pulled a cigarette out, lit it up and inhaled. It calmed him and as he exhaled, he looked down at my cherubic face that looked back at him without saying a word.

"Where the fuck is your mother?" he asked.

"She's sleeping." I replied.

Rolando was instantly agitated as he took a seat, thinking. Then, he looked back down at me.

"Hey, you want to help me do something?" he asked. I simply nodded in agreement. I had no choice but to agree. I'd seen the result of Rolando's temper. It was frequently written all over my mother's face, when the pair didn't see eye to eye, in the form of welts and bruises.

There was even a time when a happy gathering at the apartment turned ugly. One of Rolando's cousins had just been released from prison. The night saw tons of billowing smoke in the air from cigarettes and weed burning, along with bottles of all types of liquor. One thing led to another and, suddenly, a fight broke out. Some friend of Rolando's cousin was getting out of line with Mildred. Without saying a word, Rolando went into the kitchen, opened a drawer and reached for a butter knife. He proceeded to walk up to this gentleman and violently jam the knife into his cheek.

"Get my scale from the closet." Rolando instructed.

I quickly ran off to a closet near the front door and opened it. There, on the floor, was a white colored digital scale in a box. It was lifted during a pharmacy robbery several years prior; Rolando often bragged about a friend that gave it to him. Ro saw it as his special, lucky scale. It was his "money-maker", as he would call it, or better yet his "mamacita." As I retrieved the scale, Rolando had already begun to pour the weed into an aluminum tray and break it down. This was a tedious process which consisted of removing seeds and branches from the buds.

The all-too-familiar smell was pungent as I took a small whiff. It was sad; at five years old, I knew what it was.

Early in any given morning it would linger in the kitchen as I would fix myself a bowl of cereal or oatmeal.

"Today, I'm going to give you a lesson in bagging." Rolando said, the words exuberantly coming out of his mouth. He probably thought it was a kind of special bonding moment for an elder and a youngster.

The reality was, I may well have learned something at home because my mother was often sleeping, not home, or strung out high on heroin. ACS often visited Mildred, even threatened to remove my brother and I from the household, until my grandmother stepped in one day and took the initiative of enrolling us in school herself. My grandmother knew her daughter was a fuck-up. She had no ambitions in life other than to sit at home and collect a fat check from welfare. The money would be spent on beer or Marlboro cigarettes, and little snacks I'd be able to prepare on my own.

As I plopped the scale on the table and grabbed a seat next to Rolando, he simply looked at me with a grin on his face.

"Here, put this on. You don't want your fingers to smell, or turn green," he instructed as he handed me a pair of white latex gloves. I slowly put them on as I watched Rolando place a pinch of weed on the scale, half a gram to be exact.

"These are going to be nicks. They sell for five dollars, you understand?" he asked.

I often looked back at that day and notched the amount of weed as being generous, sign of the times I guess. After Rolando had asked me if I understood, I made the mistake of nodding, which in turn made Rolando snap.

"You got that? Yes or no? Don't nod your fucking head!" He shouted.

"Yes, Ro... I mean, Papi." I muttered.

For a split second, I was about to call Rolando by his name. Rolando hated that. It was yet another pet peeve of his or maybe just an excuse to just release some anger. Even though he wasn't my biological father, he was adamant about having me address him as such. This was another lesson hard pressed onto me.

••••••••••

One night, I'd gotten up and went to the kitchen for something to drink. While passing by the closed bedroom door to my mother's room, I could hear what seemed to be intoxicated giggling and moaning filling the apartment.

I grabbed a chair and placed it near the sink to reach

for a plastic sippy cup. I turned on the faucet and

filled the cup with water. I eventually drank half and

poured the rest out. It was then I remember being

enthralled at the sight of a roach trying to climb up

and out of the basin. So, I decided to fill the cup again

and proceeded to pour it on the critter.

It became this weird game because the roach was

feverishly trying not to go down the drain and I

couldn't get it to as easily as I thought it would. It

took about ten minutes until it finally went down

along with a few remaining grains of rice and beans

that were in the sink. As I went to place the cup back

in the dish rack, I managed to knock over a glass that

fell to the floor and shattered into pieces.

Suddenly, rumbling noises came from the bedroom

as the door flung open. It was Rolando, shirtless with

boxers and flip-flops on, and holding a .38 caliber gun in his hand. He ran into the kitchen in a huff as I quickly jumped off the chair and nervously awaited Rolando to enter the kitchen.

"What the fuck is going on here?" He yelled.

"I was thirsty, so I got a drink of water and the glass fell and broke." My words came out in a whimper.

My wanna-be father just stood in front of me, his half erect cock poking out through the opening in his boxers. Rolando then shook his head as if disappointed in, but forgiving for what had transpired.

"Boy, I thought some maricon had broken a window trying to rob us and shit. Listen, just go back to your room. I'll have your mother clean this mess up," he said.

I took this as a good sign at first and let out a huge sigh of relief. I was headed to my room and trailed off with, "Sorry, Rolando."

Rolando must have heard this and quickly turned towards me.

"Hold the fuck up. What did you just say? Get back here boy! What the fuck did you just call me?" He yelled out loud.

The sound of his angered voice scared the shit out of me. I could feel a knot starting to form in my throat as my body began to tremble in fear. Rolando yanked me by the arm and pulled me closer towards him.

"How many times have I told you to call me Papi? You think I'm playing games, you little shit?" He shouted.

Mildred came running into the kitchen to see what all the commotion was about. As she was opening her mouth the slightest, she was quickly cut off by Rolando.

"Don't even say a fucking word, bitch!" He screamed at her.

Making matters worse, Rolando now stuck the barrel of the gun square in my face. It was the first time I had seen a pistol up close and personal.

"You think you're tough?" Rolando asked.

"No Papi, I'm not!" I pleaded.

"Don't I try to give you and your mother everything?"
He asked menacingly.

"I'm sorry," I pleaded again.

Tears were beginning to swell in my eyes. I'd seen this deranged look coming from Rolando in the past, right before he would beat up my mother. Without

thought, Rolando backslapped me across the face. It

wasn't hard, but it was effective. He then directed me

towards the broken glass on the floor.

"Stand right there!" He ordered.

I was about to learn why always walking around the

apartment barefoot was a bad habit, in the most

painful of manners. I tried my damnedest to move my

foot, making it look like I was abiding by Rolando's

wishes, but couldn't. I was frozen with fear. This only

made Ro angrier. He finally grabbed me and moved

me closer towards the glass. He then placed the gun

right to my head and screamed, "Step on it!"

"Papi, please no, I'm sorry, I mean it!" I wailed.

"Now you want to call me Papi? You're fucking

gonna learn the hard way!" Rolando screamed.

"Please, Papi, no!"

"Step on it!"

I had no other choice. I raised my tiny left foot,
ready to press down on a decent sized shard of glass,
when I was abruptly stopped by Rolando. Deep
inside I foolishly thought Rolando had come to his
senses. I kept thinking this tough love episode was
perhaps a mere test to scare me into calling him dad
on a regular basis… Not quite.

"Do it with the right one. Put your right foot on it!"
Rolando yelled.

It was an obvious nod towards his personal
demons regarding his own handicap.

I raised my right foot and pressed down on the
glass. I still hadn't gone down all the way. I was
hoping Rolando might think it was fully pressed and
leave me alone. Rolando made sure though.

He placed his flip flop right on top of my foot and pressed down. The crunch of the glass underneath echoed in the kitchen. The screams of pain followed. Blood began seeping from under my foot as I cried hysterically. Rolando then placed his hand around my mouth and squeezed.

"If you ever call me Rolando again, I swear to God, I will fucking kill you," he threatened.

With that, he let me go. I remember quickly falling to the floor, my underfoot a bloody mess. Mildred then ran over trying to console me as best she could, but the damage had been done. This man, who she decided to bring into our home, had finally turned his rage towards her son as well. I always felt as if we were at the mercy of Rolando's sudden outbursts.

....

I watched intently, soaking up everything Rolando was doing: the separation process, the weighing. Rolando took out a crumpled brown bag, inside were hundreds of little plastic bags. "I'm going to call you the bagger man. Check it. Grab that piece and put it inside the bag" he said.

I obliged, putting the half gram of weed inside the bag. Not bad for a fist timer. One after the other, little nicks were made, which took care of one ounce. The next ounce was weighed a little more on the scale. This one would account for ten dollar bags. Finally, the last ounce, twenty sacks. It took about three hours on a Saturday afternoon, but I was well on my way to a bright future.

···········

It was funny to me how adults behaved. As a child, you really have no say in many things. I was always trying my best to refrain my tongue from pronouncing a hard roll of the letter R, as to not say Rolando. Yet, he went from calling me boy, to bagger man. I do admit, any beatings I received from that afternoon on weren't as harsh or severe as the glass incident. On the other hand, my mother suffered immensely, much of it self-inflicted because of her addiction. The drugs seemed to consume her life, and Rolando just kept feeding it to her. My days and nights were filled with different people in the apartment, mixing and mingling. The end result would always be half of them laid out on the floor or the sofa, high out of their fucking minds.

Rolando would smoke the occasional joint, but nothing more. The rest of his time was spent on observing everything. He knew his shit was potent and, sometimes, deadly. The people in the crib and on the streets, that bought it were hooked for real. At the age of seven, Rolando had already let me try some of his weed. Just a few pulls here and there. He taught me that I had to at least know what it felt like, whether it was strong or mild, to know if I was purchasing some good shit. Nice advice for a fucking seven-year-old, huh? Only to be applied to the marijuana. The heroin? That was a whole different ball game.

Chapter 2

"Mildred"

This is how the story went, the many times my mother would tell me herself. Mildred Cepeda was once this young, vibrant, beautiful girl, but would eventually turn into every parent's worst nightmare. At the young age of twelve years old, she'd begun drinking and smoking. At thirteen, she'd lost her virginity. It finally ended with her dropping out of high school and becoming a welfare mother. Mildred let her entire life sink to rock bottom and let it stay there. Long gone were the days of frilly Easter dresses and pony tails; all it took was one hot and turbulent summer to change her forever.

Her parents were Gustavo and Louisa Cepeda, descendants of the Caracol people from Guanaja, Honduras. They made their trek to America in the early sixties and settled in the South Bronx. For the most part, Mildred was given a decent upbringing, along with her younger brother, Chester. The early years saw her excel in school, developing a knack for knowing the content because she was so focused and smart.

Then puberty hit.

The year was 1968. Mildred was slowly developing into a young Miss. She found herself many a night standing in front of her mirror, simply staring at her body. It was those awkward stages in a girl's life when everything inside her body either felt weird or tingly. Puberty was validated for her when, on various occasions, she would wake up in the morning with her panties wet. Mildred would quickly have to look in her drawers and change clothes. Her hormones were raging and she didn't have a clue.

Puberty was hitting this poor girl full steam ahead, much of it in her breasts; they were becoming more and more difficult to hide. Her father, like many a man, still saw her as his little baby. He would often get into shouting matches with his wife over dressing their daughter 'down'. The result was Mildred looking like a regular at church, not showing even a hint of ankle.

The constant arguing between Mildred and her father over things like her clothes was beginning to seem routine. It would end with the young girl running into her bedroom and locking the door. She would then crank up the volume on her radio and listen to music. Her weakness was listening to love songs, like Marvin Gaye and Tami Terrell's "Ain't Nothing Like the Real Thing." It was a favorite of hers that would make her cry. It was a way to let out her emotions when she wasn't feeling good, or when her dad got on her case. It was also when she would think about... Troy.

Troy Roberts was a next-door neighbor and her best friend. The two grew up together in the same building; project-living, sometimes had its advantages. There was always someone on the same floor looking to borrow some spices, or a cup of sugar. In the summertime, the mothers from whatever floors would convene in the courtyard near the playground. After seeing the same faces together repeatedly over time, people would eventually talk.

With Mildred, her brother Chester, and Troy, the gossip had to do with a favor that would turn into a friendship.

Troy's mother was Adina Roberts. She was this single black woman that arrived in New York fresh off a bus from Richmond County, Georgia after her marriage had gone sour. She had moved into the building two years after the Cepeda's did and resided in apartment 12B, right next door to the couple. Adina struggled trying to raise a child by herself and sacrificed the best she could to get by, finally able to land a job as a nurse at Bronx Lebanon Hospital.

One night, a loud knock was heard on the Cepeda's apartment door. Adina desperately explained to them she was given a chance to work the night shift at her job with a little extra pay. Her dilemma was not having someone to stay with her son who was six at the time.

This would have been a tall order for any person to deal with, but my grandparents were different, my mother would explain. They were very understanding. They knew Adina had no family in New York and the majority of her friends were all co-workers at the hospital. Adina begged and pleaded, even offering money for the care of her child, but the Spanish couple would have none of it. They took on the duties with open arms.

This evolved into a routine that lasted for years, one that was reciprocated by Adina during the day. While the couple worked, she was the one to take the children to school and later pick them up.

As Mildred and Troy got older, they shared the benefit of attending the same schools, and even being in the same classes. They would spend hours upon hours, back and forth, from one apartment to the next. Mildred's father, Gustavo, sometimes made references of having two sons, and that's how he came to treat the boy. Gustavo knew that having a father figure in a boy's life was important, and he served that role. He cared for Troy, showed love for him. He never imagined that his only daughter and new found son would grow up having feelings for each other — at least physically.

Mildred and Troy had become the best of friends, exchanging stories about the transitions happening to their bodies, as it if was nothing out of the ordinary. They were comfortable with each other. And as time went by, their childlike innocence would also change.

Games like hide-and-seek had slowly turned into 'show me yours and I'll show you mine.' It gradually stepped up to kissing and over the clothes light petting. It culminated into her fondling his genitals and she being finger fucked routinely.

On certain occasions, Troy would sneak and read his mother's medical books, which had illustrations of body parts and their functions. They both found it amusing and exciting at the same time. It became a thrill for them to come home and head directly to Mildred's bedroom. They acted out what they saw in magazines and on television, pretending to be full adults living together. While Troy brought the books, Mildred began sneaking a cigarette here and there from her father, who smoked two packs a day. One or two loose ones wouldn't be missed. She quietly poured little cups of her father's whiskey, wanting to taste what it was all about.

As Mildred celebrated her thirteenth birthday, it was apparent her feelings for Troy were deepening. Everything seemed to be a blur around her, not even the events of the world or her city were a match to ground Mildred's thoughts. She was in a fantasy world, while New York City was in turmoil. The year of '68 already saw teacher and sanitation worker strikes, while violence was at an all-time high, my mother would always tell me. Her parents were even struggling, needing to take on second jobs just to stay afloat. This left more freedom for Mildred to be alone with Troy, and that's all she thought about — being alone with Troy. She could care less for the madness that was called the Bronx, or the fear everyone else had during this rough patch in its history.

All Mildred dreamt of was her first time. She envisioned it being special. Unfortunately, it never materialized into such a thing. Troy had snuck into the apartment late one night and went straight to her room. They kissed, they touched. He stuck it in with the aid of something lubricated his mother had brought home from the hospital. And just like that, Mildred wasn't a virgin anymore and neither was he.

••••••••••

My mother always had a way with words. She was madly blunt about things, talked about topics with fervor. The only problem was that many times her advice was ill conceived. While explaining the "birds and bees" to me, it sort of went something like, "Troy came over that night. He had a pretty big dick for a thirteen-year-old. We ended up fucking." In a bizarre way, I look back at those moments with her, sharing conversations in such a brash manner, as her way of showing some motherly love. Having Rolando around, I knew there was nothing my mother could do about her other problem. I witnessed that struggle every day.

I saw how she injected that junk into her arms, then the back of her legs, and in between her toes. She did that because she was concerned my grandmother was catching on to the bruises on her arms as being more than just her getting hit. I saw the effects of the drug more than once; it fully spread in her system. She would doze off watching her novellas, then magically wake up for a quick minute, like nothing was going on, only to nod off again. This was an awful and perpetual cycle she would go through until the drugs wore off. After that, it was as though she would sleep into a coma until the next day or even night, where she would just pick it up yet again.

My mother liked Frankie Lymon. She had these old-ass records of this dude singing with his group called "The Teenagers". She knew many of the songs word-for-word. I always saw it as ironic that she enjoyed his music; she would eventually die due to complications brought on by the drug, just like he did. Man, that fucking heroin.

•••••••••

Adina Roberts slowly moved up the ranks at the hospital until she was given the title of Head Nurse. She knew it was a job that brought along much responsibility, but she was eager for the challenge. She trudged along to work every night with no worries, even though the South Bronx must have been a battlefield. It was filled with various gangs of soldiers, and the drugs were the ammo inserted into needles, vials and bags. All of it just prolonging the start of any hint at urban renewal.

I would never blame Ms. Roberts for what happened. She was ecstatic with her new position in the hospital. She had finally progressed to giving orders, instead of taking them. Adina had so much power in her hands and that's where the problem was. Being a head nurse, she basically had access to too many rooms and all their amenities, and she oversaw inventory on certain items in the hospital. My mother explained this to me many times. There were minor things, like aspirin and various antibiotics, to bigger stuff that, ultimately, drew Adina in. Those were the bottles of methadone and a trial drug being used for patient treatment at that time, Buprenorphine.

Even though everything was going good for her, Adina still had to struggle in order to pay bills, raise a boy and get by. So, the need for extra cash was always there. It seemed like everyone towards the beginning of the seventies, was constantly surrounded by more negative shit than positive. It was filling the streets every day. All Ms. Roberts did was succumb to it. She began exercising her stature at her job by taking home some things and having a friend of hers who knew the right people, sell it. You can get caught up in the game, I know that firsthand, but she never had any idea that her son was ambitious enough to tap into her supply.

Mildred painted the picture vividly: how Troy dashed into the apartment and headed right into her room one day. He was sweating from nervousness and excitement.

"I have to show you something." he told Mildred.

"What is it?" Mildred asked.

He then reached into his pocket and took out a strange looking bottle.

"It's called, 'I'm about to make some money'," Troy joked around.

"I'm serious Troy, what is it?" She asked him again, not amused.

"It's called Methadone. They give it to the drug addicts in the hospital to treat them," he supposedly told her.

"So, why do you have it, and where did you get it from?" Mildred quickly responded.

Troy just smiled as he walked over to Mildred's bed and sat down. He proceeded to kick off his sneakers and started un-zipping his jeans.

"I took it from my mother's bag. There was a bunch of stuff inside it, so she won't miss it, believe me. My friend Reggie says we could make some money selling it to some of the fiends in the building. What do you think?" He asked Mildred, as he continued stripping, taking off his shirt and exposing his developing chest.

"No! And, I think it's a stupid idea. That's what you want to be, a drug dealer?" She lashed out at him.

Troy just ignored her rant as he tapped on the bed, waiting for her to come over and sit next to him.

"I said, no! Besides, my mother should be back from the hospital any minute," she said.

For the last several weeks her father had been ill with some infection that landed him in the ICU. Her brother, Chester, was always alongside his mother, leaving Mildred at home by herself.

Both Mildred and Troy used this time to be together, being the two were now in separate high schools. Mildred still cared for Troy, but was slowly beginning to feel like a piece of meat. Troy made it a habit of coming over after school and just wanting to fuck, nothing more. His mother would give him an allowance, which he stopped sharing with her. High school was different and it was making Troy out to be that way too. He was hanging out more with a group of friends who she didn't care too much for.

"I'm not fucking you, Troy!" she snapped back.

"Why not?" He answered.

"I don't want to. That's why. That's all you ever want to do. You don't even call me anymore, you just barge in and expect sex," she continued.

Troy jumped off the bed and playfully grabbed her, pulling her close.

"Come on baby, it'll be good, you'll see," he told her.

"I'm not doing it Troy, and that's it!" Mildred yelled.

"Fine, whatever," he said angrily, reaching down grabbing his pants.

"Why does your mother have that stuff anyway?" Mildred asked.

"I don't know and I don't care. Can I leave it here until tomorrow, at least?" he asked Mildred.

Mildred just looked at Troy. "Do you care for me?" she asked him.

Troy let out a nervous laugh, desperately trying to pretend like he hadn't heard what she said to him, until Mildred got up in his face.

"Do you care for me, care *about* me?" She asked again.

"You know I do," he told her as he stopped smiling and looked in her eyes.

"Do you love me? Well, do you?" She pressed him harder.

Troy was quiet now. A sudden silence fell between them… "Yes, Mil. I do love you," he whispered.

When mom would tell me the tale, I knew that Troy ended up admitting to something just because she wanted to hear it, but that he would have never said on his own. I never did admit that to my mother for fear she would get pissed off and stop talking to me completely. She would continue to tell me how Troy attempted to get up from the bed, but was immediately pushed back down. She'd believed his "I love you."

"Fine, you can leave it here but just for a few. I can't let my mother find that, okay? You promise to take it with you? Do you promise?" She begged him. "Yes, I promise." Troy answered.

Then Mildred said she looked at him, she kissed him on the lips softly, and began pulling off his jeans down to his boxers.

•••••••••

My mother used to get drunk and reminisce about her childhood a lot. She always spoke about Troy with emotion. She explained to me, many times, the story of the day he left the Methadone in her room. She also told me how she would never see him after that. She resorted to blasting his new friends in school for being a bunch of degenerates who always hung out in the stairwells of the apartment building and gave him grief for how he did absolutely nothing but drink and smoke.

To push the point home, she would continue with details about how they sued to play a game called "Elevator Surfing." The boys would pry open an elevator door on whatever floor, then one of them would hop on top and ride up and down until someone else was next. They decided one night, while drunk and high, to start on the fourteenth floor of

Reggie's building. Troy jumped from one elevator to the other. The police report filed later stated his foot got tangled on one of the cables that ran alongside the car. He was left dangling off the side until the car moved and he fell down the shaft to his death.

I always knew my mom was in depression mode when I would come home and see her photo albums spread all over the floor. She would cap the night off by heading into the bathroom, with her drink and cigarettes. She would then shoot up and hop into the tub and fall asleep. It often pained me listening to my mother tell me how she slowly grew into a state of constant depression after Troy's death. She would sit for hours in her room, just listening to music. The fact that her father continued in and out of the hospital while she grieved Troy didn't help her uplift either.

The worst news came when the family found out he was suffering from emphysema eventually in addition to his lung cancer. At that time in her life, Mildred couldn't take it anymore. She sat emotionless in her room, Troy gone, her father wasting away and just stared at the bottle of Methadone. The only cruel last memory she would have of Troy.

She said her grades in school began to slip, along with her sanity. She would always return full circle back to her room—just staring. Back to the bottle that was supposed to bring Troy that elusive extra cash he was looking for along with Reggie and company.

Leading up to her first foray, where the world of a heroin aggressively closed in on her ultimate high, she did her research. It consisted of talking to one of her neighbors, a gentleman by the name of Melvin.

He was known throughout the complex as an avid user of various illegal stimulants. Mildred never hinted to him what she was planning, even throwing up a facade, not showing how low she really was. She acted as if she were doing a project for school. She convinced him that she needed to interview someone with a solid knowledge base of drugs and its effects on a person. Melvin was more than receptive. He even showed her what it was all about one day — as long as she locked the door behind her. That was his only request of her because once high, he would never be able to get up from his couch, let alone close a door.

He explained to her that Methadone was good, but the real deal was pure heroin. He showed her how one can even smoke it; all you needed was a small sheet of aluminum foil, a lighter, and a tube. Melvin liked using the cardboard tube from a paper towel roll. He could cut it into three smaller ones that would last for several uses and freebase all day. Once her prepped the platform, Melvin instructed her on how to heat the powder from underneath to produce an instant milky white vapor.

As the smoke rose, he gently placed the tube over it and inhaled. This was a scary sight for a young fourteen-and-a-half-year-old girl, she said, but it was a hard knock lesson in ghetto living. The way his eyes seemed to roll back into his head, only showing white... more than she had bargained for. "It's the fastest way to get high, Mil," he had told her, as he sat back enjoying every second.

Another method he taught her was using a syringe. He started out with a spoon and poured the heroin on it, "You have to dissolve it first. You can use water or, sometimes, I like to use lemon juice. It kind of gives it a sweet sting once you inject it." The citric acid in the juice was to help break down the drug quicker, though he emphatically stressed to Mildred this was to be done only with brown heroin.

Mildred told me how Melvin heated the spoon until it looked like it was boiling. He then showed her how to fill the syringe with every last drop of heroin from the spoon. Melvin then took off his black belt from his worn-out jeans and wrapped it around his arm so tightly that every single vein on his arm just bulged and throbbed.

"I need your help," he once told her. He wanted the girl to keep pulling on the belt as hard as she could until he was done.

The blood and heroin swirled inside the syringe, finally mixing together. He then shot it into his arm and would lean his head back. "Okay, let it go," he instructed.

His veins would settle back down as the blood and drug circulated throughout his body. Mildred observed him and watched him fall in and out of coherency. She also started to wonder what it would feel like to partake instead of just watch. At age fifteen, she did just that. Mildred was hooked on it from that point for the rest of her life.

••••••••••

My mother totally lost all hope, I guess. School was really weighing her down, she said. Reading Cyrano De Bergerac for English class wasn't a priority anymore. Roaming the halls, trying to score some drugs by offering anyone a blow-job, or a quick fuck in the staircase, seemed much more practical. I was tormented by friends, and even relatives, growing up. They teased me about my mother being this filthy and desperate drug addict whore who exchanged sex for her fixes.

She told me how she'd eventually said the hell with it and left school altogether. Living with her was rough, but not for the reasons one would think — only because she never looked happy. Her smiles about life, in general, were always few and far between. Her relationship with my grandmother was also strained, even more so when my grandfather passed away. All I ever saw were pictures of him.

At seventeen my mother was a full-blown addict. Out of fucking control. It was around this time she

met the person who is supposedly my father. They
stayed together for three years, her giving birth to me
when she was twenty. All she ever told me about him
was that he was known in her circle of friends as
Raph, short for Raphael. He was this hardcore gang
banger back in the day, claiming the "Seven
Immortals".

Other than that, who knows? By the time I was
born, he took a long walk and never came back. My
mother kept at the drugs though. It was boggling that
I was born healthy, with no kinds of side effects of her
drug use. Nothing. Rolando… Papi, would come into
her life later, around the time I was five. He was
supposed to take care of her but treated her like shit,
just the same as she was treated before. I kind of felt
sorry for her. If she ever had any goals or a passion
for something that she wanted to accomplish in life,

he would never let it happen. He made sure she

stayed high, twenty-four-seven.

•••••••••

It was a late Monday night. I would always wake up

at strange hours, thirsty. As I made my way down the

hall I had to pass by my mother and Rolando's room.

On this particular night, the door was slightly open.

My curiosity got the best of me as I slowly pushed the

door open wider. It was quiet inside, until I heard a

laugh. This brought a smile to my face. There hadn't

been many times where my mother was in a chipper

mood. I remember bursting in the room with glee,

"Mommy!" I yelled with enthusiasm. I then saw

Rolando on the bed, covered by a blanket. He

appeared to be on top of my mother.

I'd seen things like this going on before but never really knew what was actually happening. As I got closer, I looked off to the side of the bed and saw my mother there, sitting down; her head slumped forward in a drug-induced stupor. Rolando looked over at me and simply put his index finger on his lips, hushing, "Just go get your drink and get back to bed, boy." He would tell me. I slowly turned around and headed back towards the hallway. As I reached the door, I turned back and took one last look at the bed, at my mother on the floor. The only image embedded in my mind was the blanket slowly moving up and down, wrapped around Rolando and... someone else.

....

I was eight years old when my brother was born. Poor son of a bitch, he suffered the full force of my mother's substance abuse. My mom kept using, smoking cigarettes, and drinking well into her pregnancy. You would think for the life of God, knowing a living being is inside your body, that a person would do everything in her power to ensure that a pregnancy went smoothly with no complications. Not my mom. Giving birth wasn't a priority. She didn't give a fuck, neither did Rolando. Hell, the day he found out he was having a kid, he celebrated with a bunch of friends, drinking and fucking some bitch he met, as he poetically put it.

I tried dealing with my baby brother, but it was difficult. My grandmother did the bulk of the work by raising him during the week. I saw Miguel on the weekends. All I could think of was the uncontrollable screaming out of nowhere and the noises he made rocking back and forth for hours. Trying to feed him was a total and definite disaster every time; on top of

everything else… that shit can really scar you.

Chapter 3

"The Paving Road"

It was 1986 and I was ten. In the last five years, I'd really learned a lot of things, only some of which a young boy my age should have known. With such dysfunctional living, it was a miracle I was even able to comprehend and grasp the teachings of academia. I did enjoy school and having friends. It was a different world outside the doors to my apartment, one that showed me the true nature of what it was to be a child. I think I embraced this part of my life dearly because I fully knew once I got back home, it was like an instant transformation in the aging process. I had to become a man and do many things on my own.

I was skilled at cooking meals, feeding myself, and my brother, and always leaving food for "Papi". I attempted to leave a plate for my mother at times, but she wouldn't eat much, often leaving the food untouched. I learned to wash clothes and iron them. I took care of Miguel, trying to show him love and understanding on the days or nights he wasn't with our grandmother.

All of this was manageable, but I still had one major influence affecting this other world of mine: the drugs. Rolando taught it to me with reckless abandon. There was a contrived list of rules in drug etiquette, processed and to live by, and Rolando saw this as a game of sorts. He would try and catch me off guard with questions every once in a while. He would throw them out at random and I would stand up straight and answer, as if a cadet in the military.

"What should you always know about your weed?" Rolando grilled.

"Crystals are important. The more you see, the better the weed," I fired back.

"What else?" he would then ask.

"For the most part, it should be green. Other colors may be acceptable but mostly green. It should be sticky and not crumbled easily. Weed that has too many seeds and branches is a waste of time, probably not good to smoke either," I'd yell out.

After some time, I rattled off these rules as if reciting my own name. I knew them forwards and backwards. Sadly, what started out as something twisted and forced became what I began to like. It became fun for me, especially the fact that Rolando didn't seem like a tyrant or some asshole anymore during this discourse. He was this father-figure I so desperately wanted and needed. I embraced it only because my mother wasn't much of a factor in my life and, no matter what Rolando was showing me, whether good or bad, someone was actually spending time with me.

One Friday evening, Rolando sat in the kitchen, a half-lit Viceroy dangling from his mouth. He had an opened forty-ounce of Budweiser on the table. Next to the beer was mamacita, along with a notepad and a pencil. The rest of the table was filled with an assortment of money in separate piles. There were stacks of fives, tens, twenties, and fifties. Rolando went over each stack and counted them several times, then notated the dollar amounts on his pad.

This particular time I strolled into the kitchen and just stopped in front of the table, without saying a word. I remember focusing on the money with a fascinated look on my face. Rolando took a pull from his cigarette as he looked at me.

"What are you doing?" he asked.

"Nothing," I answered while shrugging my shoulders.

"Where did your mother go?" Rolando questioned. "She went to abuelita's house to get Miguel," I answered.

"Ah, shit! She's bringing that little fuck here tonight? I told her I have people coming over," he snickered angrily.

I began pulling out a chair from the table in order to sit down.

"Don't worry, I'll take care of him, Papi," I remember saying.

"Good, I don't think I'd be able to deal with his nonsense tonight," Rolando said unsympathetically.

Rolando then slowly gathered the money, collecting the fifties first and working down.

"Can I ask you a question, Papi?" I then asked him.

"What is it?" he answered with a stern look on his face.

"Do your friends have money like you?" I asked him.

"What do you mean?" Rolando said. He was confused.

"I see you give some of your friend's money, so do they have as much as you do?" I then clarified.

"No. They work for me. I'm the man that pays them." Rolando said, puffing his chest in a machismo type fashion.

"What about me, does that mean I work for you then?" I asked.

"You slick son of a bitch. What is this all about? You want money? That's why you're asking me all these questions?" Rolando said. A slight grin was beginning to form.

"No, Papi. No," I said nervously.

"Hey. Don't be scared. I like that, okay? Don't ever be afraid to speak what's on your mind. I know I treat you a certain way, but it's for a reason. First of all, you never tell anyone what I've shown you, or what you know, is that clear? Secondly, never let anyone bitch you out. Take advantage of you, you know? You always be up front and direct. Around here it's different because this is my house and you must obey the rules in it. I'm talking outside, you know, when you're with your friends. There's always going to be a time to fool around and there is a time to be serious, make that money. I treat you tough because I want you to grow up and be a leader, have all your friends following you around. You hear me?" He spoke

defiantly.

I just sat there, letting the words penetrate my

thoughts. Suddenly, I looked over at Rolando more

rebellious than I'd ever felt in my life.

"Can I get some money for sneakers?" I asked

Rolando.

"Why?" Rolando quickly shot back.

I fidgeted some but was immediately stopped by

Rolando.

"What I say? Be direct. Have no fear," he told me.

"My friends make fun of my sneakers. That's why I

want new ones. The good ones, so that I can be cool,

and everybody will like me." I told him after thinking

for a few seconds.

My money ploy had much to do with the cheap

and dirty imitation sneakers my mother would buy

me, when she felt like shopping. Rolando immediately looked down at my feet. True to my word, my sneakers appearance was sadly played out.

"You think a pair of new sneakers is going to make you popular?" Rolando spoke.

"No. But, how am I supposed to be a leader if they make me feel bad? If I always look like a bum?" I said.

"Fuck them! Your attitude should be 'fuck you' to anyone and everyone, especially your friends. You hear me? But, I know where you're coming from. It's like a competition. And a bum certainly isn't going to win any competition looking the way they do. So, yeah—if one of your friends has something nice, then you have to go and get something else that's nicer. If they have money in their pockets, always have more. That's how you're going to be a leader. Let me ask you something. What kind of sneakers do you want?" Rolando said.

"I want Jordans!" I shouted out with a smile.

Rolando quickly let out a burst of laughter. "Damn little man, those things are like a hundred and forty or fifty dollars. That's what you want? That's what you really want? Okay, you got them. We'll go tomorrow," he agreed.

I leaped off my chair and pumped my fist. Then I bolted out of the kitchen with a wild sense of happiness. Rolando once told me that after I exited that day, he sat there in the kitchen with a smile of his own. He whispered to himself that I was ready, it seemed. Ready to be taken to the next level.

•••••••••

I was ten years old and going to school with cash in my pockets. I would buy the latest video games, the best clothes. If I was hungry, I ate whatever I wanted. I remember going to school with my new Jordans on, my friends sick with envy. I was finally able to rid myself of all my nasty, dirty and cheap sneakers with holes in the bottom of them. When you're young, these are the things that count — material shit. I look at a lot of kids nowadays going to school and it's no different. Education is like a big fucking fashion show, everybody parading what they're wearing.

Kids will let you know, too. If you're broke, they make jokes about it. If you act a certain way, someone will spot it and shout you out. I shook in fear of getting into "Yo' Momma" rank outs. I knew I would get beat and humiliated every time, so I ended up taking Rolando's advice. I spent money, but did it wisely. I always made sure I had money left over. It made me feel important to have people hanging out with me. They looked up to me. Little did I know, Rolando was just poisoning my thoughts. He made me feel like I shouldn't trust anyone. Any friends I made weren't really there to look out for my interests, but they're own; therefore, I kept it strictly business.

It was like a competition that I always had to win somehow. The money he gave me wasn't to help my self-esteem. It wasn't because he cared. I was naive. Every child is. He made me feel important for a reason. I was a leader all right. Strategically placed by him to do his dirty work and that's exactly what happened next.

Chapter 4

"And So, the Strike Foo Canines Were Formed"

I raced home every day after school. The restlessness I felt while sitting in class was unbearable, especially in the afternoon. As the clock on the wall ticked, I anxiously waited to be released so I could be home on time for my favorite cartoon, "The Strike Foo Canines".

It was normal for me to sit in front of a television for hours while doing homework, but that particular cartoon was special. Absolutely, positively, no matter what, education was put to rest while Master Roddy Chon-Ging and crew got down to business.

I was now in middle school and the work was going to be somewhat harder and more advanced. Apart from what I was learning in class, I also maintained a steady knowledge of the "real world", as Rolando would say. He often stressed to me that getting older was only going to bring about more responsibility.

Watching this show of mine was a way to tune out, transport me into another world. A team of dog-like humans, masters in martial arts and fighting for the protection of the Earth, was a way to escape the chaotic lifestyle adulthood brought.

"Power of lightning! Power of thunder! Strike Foo Canines, onward!" I often shouted, as I held a pen in the air, pretending it was the magical blade of spirits. I would then mimic what the character of Master Roddy was doing as he battled the evil villain, General Abrax-Rah.

The next day at school, my friends and I would gather in the schoolyard and talk about the episode from the day before. We critiqued what we saw, each

of us inputting opinions on this series that captivated

our imaginations.

My circle of friends included Jose, a chubby Spanish

kid from my building who was one strong son of a

gun. With his overlapping gut and broad shoulders, it

literally took three of us to bring him down whenever

we played football in the yard. There was also Billy

"Duckie" Griffin, the only white boy in my class.

Thinking back to it, the entire school probably.

Everyone called him Duckie because of the waddling

nature of his walk.

I always had a thing for Rosemary Delgado. The

fellas accepted her in our group because she was

smart and acted like one of us. Many times, she

sashayed her Latin attitude with an exclamation mark

by puckering up her lips and shaking her head when she talked. She was very passionate in what she preached, whether during a regular conversation or in an argument. She also bragged about her older brother being a legitimate member of the Latin Kings and a threat to anyone's health, if she were ever fucked with.

There was also Tazeem Abdul Aalee Rahmini, Taz for short. He was one of my best friends along with Duckie and Jose. Tazeem's mother was Puerto Rican, while his father was one of those militant black men, always yapping about pro-black, anti-white and an avid member of the N.O.I, the Nation of Islam.

Some of those teachings rubbed off on Taz. One of them I quickly observed was the fact that Taz would never hold a cigarette or joint, throw up a middle finger, or anything, with his right hand. He would reserve those kinds of things and actions for his left hand. It was always something that intrigued me about him, but I never really brought the topic up in a full-blown discussion.

With all the preachy rhetoric coming from his father's mouth, Taz was also one of those children that seemed brainwashed into believing everyone was always against the black man. He let those emotions fly one day by hurling a book at the white librarian in school and was suspended for doing so. His father got involved and caused a raucous over the incident, threatening to sue everyone and their mother if his child wasn't let back in. Somehow the school officials listened and, needless to say, Taz was allowed back in school immediately.

Then there was Monifa, and her brother Carl. Monifa was the apparent smart one as Carl was a year older and still in the seventh grade. He was one of those Special-ED students that the group used to make fun of, insinuating his classes were in the school's basement and boiler room. Monifa and her brother were at constant odds with each other, forever arguing about the littlest things. The fights would last several minutes until out of nowhere, everything seemed to be cool between them.

Finally, there was Abraham, the studious one out of all of them. He was considered to be the nerd of the group, but I liked him just the same. I always kept him close, knowing well that Abraham was my ultimate ticket out of junior high school.

The eight of us bonded together, always offering protection for one another. We were known throughout the school as "The Strike Foo Crew." Jerome Avenue and its surroundings were ours to defend from any and all types of threats. We each played along, relating the cartoon characters to ourselves. Me being the leader and all, I had to be Master Roddy Chon-Ging. Jose used his brute strength, as did his counterpart, Captain Barry Bull. Rosemary was the quick-footed and always deadly Nanjitsa Chow, with Abraham representing the lovable and smart Pug-Pug. Duckie was one who loved confrontation, and boy could he get down if in a fight. Therefore, he took on the role of Shar-Payne. Monifa and Carl were supposed to be the sibling duo of Shia-Tzu and her brother Ryu-Tzu. And then there was Taz. Unfortunately, the elite team of The Strike Foo Canines were all sewed up in we seven, which only meant one thing. Due to his mean streak and last name of Rahmini, it was a no-brainer. We all knew Taz had to be the one and only General Abrax-Rah.

"Blade of spirits, guide us with your visions," I shouted at the television one day as I got my daily fix.

Master Roddy held his sword up to the sky and with it was able to see an army of mutants forming together and heading towards his team. I watched intently, waiting for the action to start. Suddenly, I heard a loud crashing noise coming from the kitchen. I quickly got off the bed and lowered the volume on my set. There was an interval of silence until I heard another round of what appeared to be glass shattering. I opened the door to my room with trepidation and my trusty sword of spirits equivalent—pen in hand.

Boom! Crash! More noise came from the kitchen. As I walked down the hallway, the scurrying noise was getting louder. I finally peeked in only to see my mother standing on a chair about to step onto the counter. She frantically threw everything from the cupboards onto the kitchen floor. It was already a mess with broken glasses and dishes, mixed with sugar, oatmeal packets and canned goods. She had a deranged look in her eyes, as if possessed.

"Mom, what are you doing?" I asked her.

"Get the hell out of here. Go back to your fucking room!" she yelled.

Even though I asked, I knew exactly what my mother was doing. I'd seen her this way before. She was dripping with sweat from the exertion and her hair was a mess. "I know he hid that shit, I just know it!" She ranted.

At that point, she leaped off the chair with way too much energy. It was fueled by her rabid need for a heroin fix. She searched everywhere in the room, above cabinets and below. Mildred then stopped and looked over at me.

"Do you know where it is?" she asked.

"I don't know what you're talking about," I answered back, pretending to be clueless.

She then screamed out, "That motherfucker, where did he put it?!"

Mildred stormed out of the kitchen now. I waited there, but my eyes were focused on the cupboards. I knew what she was looking for and to my detriment, I knew where it was. I'd spent so much time in the kitchen with Rolando that I was well aware of every hiding spot Rolando used for his drugs.

I continued waiting until I heard my mother attacking her bedroom with the same intensity. I knew I'd only have a short window of opportunity to climb on the chair and retrieve what she was so

desperately seeking. So, I made my move.

I climbed on the chair and onto the counter. I had to

tippy toe, holding onto the front of the cupboards for

support. With my right hand, I was able to open the

cabinet door and I used my pen to move a can of soup

from the highest shelf off to the side. In the back was

a bag of flour. I stretched out my arm as best as I

could. Once again, using my pen to try and move the

flour but couldn't; I decided to puncture the bag with

it. I now stuck the pen inside the hole and slowly

started moving the flour bag forward. It was working.

I slid the bag right near the ledge of the shelf, but

there was no way I was going to be able to hold it in

my hands. I was already beginning to feel pain and

weakness in my feet for having tippy toed for so long.

My only move left was to let the bag of flour fall to

the floor. As it came crashing down, a smoke of white

filled the air and instantly fogged up the entire

kitchen. The crash wasn't loud at all, but I was

hurrying nonetheless before my mother could

reappear back in the kitchen.

I quickly jumped off the counter and looked inside

the flour bag. In it was a zip lock bag with a piece of

tape marked Z, Mister Blackstone. I knew what it was

immediately. The Z was representative of an ounce.

The name Mister Blackstone indicated it was brown

heroin. It looked uncut. Rolando had it stashed

because he was going to break it down into little bags

for selling, or he was going to sell the whole ounce. It

was plain to see that no matter which, he was hiding

it from prying hands, those being my mother's.

I quickly grabbed the bag and headed out of the kitchen but to my dismay, Mildred just stood there at the entrance watching me.

"What do you have in your hands?" she asked.

"Nothing!" I fired back.

"Don't you lie to me. Don't you fucking lie to me!" Mildred screamed as she lunged forward.

Mildred rushed to me and violently grabbed me by the arm, raising it. She saw the bag and her eyes widened.

"Let me get it!" She screamed out.

"Get off of me!" I screamed back, flailing my arms trying to break free from her grip.

"Just let it go you little shit," she ranted.

I have to admit at that point I was scared. So many times, I'd seen my mother shooting up. So many times, I'd seen the results of the heroin in her system.

This was a first, her maddening attempt to snatch this bag from me so she could get high; it was a different person that had taken over her body.

"Mom, please, let go of me!" I begged her.

"Just drop the bag!" She ordered.

The confrontation then worsened. Mildred raised her hand in the air and brought it down with pure rage, smacking me right in the face. My head ferociously snapped back, my cheek instantly turned red from the blow. Whatever daze I was now in, however fast I was trying to recuperate from the slap, was short lived. My mother did it again.

It was anger, sadness, humiliation, and fear. It was every pent-up emotion I had ever lived with that rose from my stomach and into my eyes, welling them with tears. I finally pushed my mother and screamed, "Get the fuck off of me!"

Mildred flew backwards into the table and fell to the floor. I had finally struck my own mother. In that instant, I realized what I had become. I was the typical man my mother always dealt with throughout her life: the user, cheater, abuser, and beater. I didn't mean to, nor did I want to. I had no other choice. I was defending myself, fearing for my life.

I quickly ran out of the kitchen and into my bedroom, locking the door behind me. I was terrified, crying hysterically. There was really no place to hide. A brain has only so much time to react in certain situations. I chose my room probably out of comfort but, really, I knew I'd cornered myself. The only option left was for me to slide underneath my bed and close my eyes, just wanting this day, this particular moment in time, to erase itself completely.

I clenched tightly to the bag and prayed, "God, please make her stop, please just make her stop." I repeated this over and over again.

Boom!

Mildred banged on the door from outside.

"Open up this fucking door right now!" she yelled.

"Leave me alone!" I screamed as I kept my eyes shut, hiding my head in my arms.

Mildred continued banging on the door incessantly. The knocks seemed to echo in my ears. They were getting louder and louder, harder and harder. Mildred must have stood outside like a crazed lunatic with balled up fists, trying her damnedest to get in. With each pound on the door I remember flinching in fear, and still there was no definite answer from God.

I remember covering my ears. I tried anything to block out the horrible sound. "Please God, I promise I will do anything, just make her stop," I prayed again. I know I was sincere and passionate about my plea. When suddenly, I felt a calm come over me. I felt relaxed and unafraid. The banging had stopped like magic.

I was young but at that age I still had some kind of faith in a higher being. I prayed at night before going to bed, asking for forgiveness for what Rolando was teaching me. I asked for my mother to get better one day, for my brother to be like any other normal boy, I would follow my grandmother's model by making the sign of the cross every time we passed Woodlawn Memorial cemetery on a bus ride back to my apartment. I would even go to church with her on occasions, always asking to light the candle after she'd donated.

I felt relieved. For the first time, God had truly answered my prayer by bringing a silver lining to such a dark cloud that always hovered in my apartment. I slowly began to slide out from under the bed. After all my praying and crying, I looked down at my hand and remembered the reason for all the drama. I still held onto the bag of Mister Blackstone. Wiping the tears away from my face, I then massaged my cheek. Surprisingly, the sting was also gone. A faint smile began to form on my face as I stared at the door.

I was beginning to feel relaxed; suddenly, the door flew open, kicked by Mildred's dirty foot. She quickly ran into the room, grabbed me by my hair and pulled me down to the floor. She then proceeded to finally yank the bag from my hand.

··········

I remember that day many times throughout my life. How my mother attacked me and tried to get the bag of heroin from my hands. I had never dreamt of talking back to my mother when I was little, let alone puttin' my hands on her. And despite my fucked upbringing, despite my mother being this drug addict, even though her man was a coward and a piece of shit, I was the one that felt bad that day.

It's just that once you raise your hand for the first time, that's all it takes. All respect for that person fails to exist from then on. She took the heroin from me and locked herself in her room.

Rolando later found out and dealt with her on his own. Me on the other hand, I was commended for putting up a fight, even though she got the bag from me anyway. Rolando saw that I could be trusted, that I had heart to stand up and protect the product. It showed a sense of toughness and character. That I would get down for mine, if I had to. He asked me about my friends; how I felt about them; whether they looked up to me. I told him they would certainly listen and that was good enough. He said I showed leadership qualities. "If they listen, they will do," he said.

He thought the whole Foo Crew thing was cute. He asked me who else was tough in the group. I told him Jose, Duckie, and Taz. "That's your team," he said. I didn't know what he was talking about. I enjoyed the 'Strike Foo Canines'. I thought they were cool as shit back then. I look back now on my life and I see this weird connection I had with the character of Master Roddy. You see, for a cartoon show it was great. It was what every child wanted to see. Tons of action and super powers, weird creatures, it was good versus evil. But the real story behind the show was quite perplexing for a child my age to really grasp. It wasn't until much older that I kind of broke the show down.

···········

It was during the year 751, the army of the Tang Dynasty had been defeated by an army of the Nanzho Empire, led by an evil general by the name of Abra. During this brief battle, an ancient temple had been ruined. Deep within the walls of this temple a magical box was hidden that contained ten powerful amulets. Eight of these amulets resembled various dogs called Foo Dogs or sometimes referred to as the lion dog.

They were guardian breeds: Chongqing, Chow Chow, Pug, Shar Pei, Bull Pei, and a Shih Tzu. The general of course had gotten hold of this box which meant destruction in the worst of terms if it were used in the wrong way. This brought upon the assembling of an elite team of fighters to seek out and retrieve the amulets.

General Abra had combined the power of these amulets which then opened a portal. Right before his wicked rendition of incantations and yelling, the Strike Force jumped on the scene and yet another battle ensued. While fighting, the amulets were separated as everyone was sucked into this portal and warped through time into the future. The strike members all grabbed onto one amulet each, transforming them into the dog depicted. The general held onto another transforming him into a dangerous demon being, with the final amulet lost somewhere on Earth.

Traveling through this portal, the journey lasted several years. Not only did the strike force transform, but they also aged in the process. The strike force realized they were still these youngsters that were trapped inside the bodies of older soldiers.

•••••••••

I felt like I was kind of the opposite. I was this man, still inside the body of a little child. For my twelfth birthday, Rolando gave me an ounce of marijuana, already prepared in nickel bags. He said, "Make it happen."

I took it to school.

The Strike Foo Crew officially had work to do.

Chapter 5

"Small Fries. Big Business."

Towards the latter part of the eighties, many schools throughout the city were introduced to the idea of installing metal detectors. One by one we'd enter the building and were subjected to an array of sounds that consisted of beeps and buzzers. If you were one of the lucky ones, you were pulled out of line and scanned individually by a handheld machine. Your friends didn't make it any easier. There were taunts of, "Check for the knife in his backpack," or an instant classic, "He's got a gun… inside his ass."

Nobody complained though. I mean we couldn't. There was no hollering of privacy invasion or racial profiling back then. We were all culprits. It was like entering a courthouse or an airport. Funny thing is, we might as well have been flying, because the weed I started pumping in school had motherfuckers high as kites.

....

I'd wake up at seven o'clock in the morning every day. It was a routine that included brushing my teeth, taking a piss, finally getting dressed and then making something to eat for breakfast. Once the money came, the latter part of this daily ritual was spent purchasing bacon, eggs, and cheese on a toasted bagel along with a small carton of orange juice to wash it down. Baller status.

I remember, the first day I was supposed to go to school with weed, I was up earlier than usual. I'd spent the night tossing and turning, feeling a bit

jittery.

I woke up that morning and took care of my

business in the bathroom. Then I walked into my

room and threw on my clothes, which had been

neatly draped over a chair and ironed. I slipped into a

pair of Jordans, the newest ones in the shoe line at the

time. My sneakers had to be laced a certain way as

well. Starting at the top loops, I would skip one and

work down and then tie the laces up, loosely at that.

This method ensured that I would never have to untie

my sneakers in order to put them on or take them off.

I would simply stick my foot inside the shoe and keep

it moving.

Now I was ready. I looked at myself in the mirror,

making sure the baseball cap I was wearing just had a

bit of a tilt to it. I then threw my book bag over my

shoulder and was headed for my first day of work. Everything seemed right as I strolled by my mother's bedroom towards the front door, until I heard my mother say, "I know what you're about to do."

I stopped abruptly and waited. I then slowly backed up and pushed open my mother's bedroom door. Mildred lay on the bed, staring at me as I entered.

"Good morning, mom," I said to her.

Mildred slowly turned over and sat up. She placed her pillow in back of her and leaned against it. Mildred's appearance was starting to take a turn for the worst. She was losing weight; her breasts were beginning to sag dramatically and her eyes seemed dark and sunken in. It's as if her soul was being sucked from her with each passing day.

She reached over, grabbed her pack of Marlboros and took one out. She lit the cigarette and took a pull from it as she looked at me, "Rolando told me what

he gave you. You're never going to amount to

anything like that."

Without any hesitation, I answered her back with a

brash, "Like you care."

The words came out of my mouth freely as

Mildred continued sitting there, emotionless. Her

arms were exposed, as I now looked them up and

down. I could see the bruised track marks from all her

injection sites.

I scanned her legs and saw more of the same.

Towards her right ankle there appeared to be a nasty

looking scab, which Mildred began to pick at until it

bled. It was annoying to me, watching my mother

pick at her body, or the constant scratching fits she

would go through. Mildred would almost constantly

scratch at her arms, her neck, then cycle back to her arms again.

"Why don't you care, mom? Why don't you care about Miguel and me? You say that I won't amount to anything, but what did you do that was so special? What have you done in life that I can look at and be proud of?" I said as I started to raise my voice. Mildred just stared at me as she continued taking pulls from her cigarette until I finally got in her face.

"You know it's true. You can't even say anything. Look at you. You're always high, you don't give a shit about anything else," I taunted.

"Shut up," she finally snapped back.

"What? Are you waiting for me to leave so that you can get high?" I yelled out.

"Shut up Antonio!" Mildred said as she began to fidget.

"I hate you. I hate you so much, mom. Why don't you go shoot up? After that, go have some fun with your man and maybe end up having another fucking retarded kid!" I added, finally garnering a reaction.

Mildred leaped off the bed and grabbed me by both of my arms. "Shut the fuck up!" She screamed out while shaking me violently and then slapping me across my face.

My words had torn into her. I could see the tears starting to swell in her eyes. "You think I wanted any of this? There is nothing I can do now! You're still young enough to turn your life around and do something good with it, instead of being a fucking drug dealer," she yelled out, immediately breaking down and crying hysterically.

"You can stop; you can get help," I said to her.

"For what? I like feeling high. Don't you understand that it is the only thing I have that numbs the pain from my pathetic life? I never wanted any of this. I'm sorry, Antonio. But I didn't want to be a mother. I didn't know how to be one. So yes, you're right, I am a failure on that part. I just don't want you to do the same," she yelled back.

I stood there quietly, Mildred still sobbing. I had bowed my head as I slowly grabbed my book bag from the floor and flung it over my shoulder. I then turned around and headed for the door and said, "Nothing is ever too late, mom. You can still change."

As I reached the door, Mildred replied, "You're wrong, Antonio. It's too late for me."

I remember turning around and looking at my mother, she had a pained look in her eyes when she added, "I'm sick, Antonio. The doctor says I have AIDS. How much do you hate me now?"

I didn't know how to react or what to say. I simply turned towards the door and exited the room. I continued heading for the front door of my apartment, desperately trying to stay strong, but I could feel myself beginning to breathe harder. The apartment felt like it was getting smaller. I tried to swallow, but it was difficult. I felt like I was choking. I finally leaned against the wall and covered my face with my hands, and simply broke down into tears.

••••••••••

It was easy getting around the whole metal detector thing. We coordinated our days, Taz, Duckie, Jose, and myself. While two would go to school early, the other two would come late. Once I had someone inside already, it was simple enough to open a back door exit or a window from a first-floor boy's bathroom. I would slip them the nick bags, and then enter school through the front doors like it was nothing.

It was amazing how many pot heads were in my school, already smoking weed and cigarettes at our age. I started out by letting some of the older kids know; suddenly, one person told another person, and so on and so on. All it took was a simple nod and a tap on the chest with two fingers out as if giving a peace sign. The teachers never knew. This was just a customary way of saying, "What's up" to a friend. We did hand-to-hands in the hallway, acted like we were giving five to someone. It was a quick exchange of money and weed.

We sold in class, underneath the table exchanges, in the lunchroom, the staircases, and the bathroom. We created a buzz, like some corporate honchos creating a market for their new product about to hit stores. The nicks were going like crazy. I gave the fellas a dollar for every bag they sold. They didn't mind. The Foo Crew was running a drug business right out of middle school.

Once I emptied out, I would run back to Rolando to re-up on more weed. He started out by cutting me some slack, but as I got more involved with selling, he began charging me regular street prices for it. This was done in order to slowly ease my transition from being a helper, to actually doing all the work by myself and selling it. I had to learn how to maximize my product, get the most money out of what I was dealing. He made me into my own boss, with my own store, my own workers.

Back when I was five, Rolando used just a half a gram to make nicks. But as time passed, more and more people started selling weed, so the price all depended on the type of shit you were selling. I had primo stuff, therefore, I was able to skimp on the amount and still charge my regular prices. Rolando charged me sixty dollars for an ounce of weed. An ounce broken down into grams was 28/35; therefore, I was able to make twenty-eight nick bags with a gram in each. The 35-part of the ounce was my personal stash; I would roll a joint from time to time to get high with the rest of the fellas. Twenty-eight bags divided by four was seven and that's how many bags we each had on our person. I had three workers who each took a dollar for every bag sold. Twenty-eight times three was eighty-four dollars, plus my thirty-five, equaled one hundred and nineteen dollars.

After buying some more stuff, I was only left with a profit of fifty-nine dollars. At first that was alright, I guess, but I would spend my profit money on stupid things like candy, food, and going to the movies. I definitely began thinking how I needed more shit to sell.

Chapter 6

"Casper and the Cutting Crew"

[OCTOBER 13, 1989

10:23 P.M.

N.Y.P.D. 75TH PRECINCT

NARCOTICS DIVISION]

LIEUTENANT HOROWITZ: "Unit 12, are you in position?"

DETECTIVE TRAMELL: "This is unit 12. Pulling up to the

corner of New Lots Ave. and Vermont St. right now."

LIEUTENANT HOROWITZ: "No one is to make a move until

suspects leave the bodega, is that understood?"

DETECTIVE TRAMELL: "Affirmative."

....

Detective Steven Tramell put the radio down near

his side. His hands were sweaty as he rubbed his

thighs to dry them. He was anxious and fidgety, as he

let out quick short breaths trying to calm down.

Tramell had just graduated to Detective. He was

working as undercover for the narcotics division out

of the 75th precinct in Brooklyn, East New York.

This night was his first bust and he was a bit antsy.

At the age of twenty-five, he was the third youngest

officer, out of the 75 to graduate and go undercover.

His partner, Detective Joshua Redding, rode next to

him and smoked a cigarette. He couldn't help but

smile upon seeing Tramell breathing, as if practicing

some Lamaze birth technique.

"You should smoke a cigarette, it'll calm you down," he told Tramell.

"I don't smoke. And would you mind lowering your window a little more, you're killing me right now," he answered as Redding just laughed and pressed on a button to lower the window.

The two detectives sat in a dark blue Buick Electra with tinted windows. They were now parked on the corner of a block near a liquor store.

Both detectives frequently eye balled their side mirrors, the rear-view mirror, out of the windows, just trying to see what was going on around them. The East New York section of Brooklyn was a haven for drugs and crime, and they were practically right in the middle of it.

The two detectives were a part of a group that included eight others and was spread throughout the neighborhood, waiting for the big bust to go down.

The main focus was a little bodega named Primo's, further down the block and across the street from where they were. For months, the store had been staked out as a major drug spot, with the help of a local informant that had befriended Redding.

Apart from the store, the detectives were tipped off on a special delivery to be made by a runner for one of the major drug suppliers in Brooklyn. Tramell quickly learned the motto from his new boss, Lieutenant James Horowitz, "In order to catch the big fish, the smaller ones had to be reeled in first."

The small fish in question this night was a black male, in his early twenties by the name of Lamont Jordan. Jordan rolled with a set called the New Lots

Terrors, or NLT for short. The gang did big business distributing all sorts of drugs throughout East New York, working out of the Louis Heaton Pink Houses near Linden Boulevard. Their tactics for intimidation in the projects were simple enough: violence.

A light drizzle now began to fall as Redding took one last pull from his cigarette and flicked it out the window. He looked at his watch. It was 10:26 P.M. yet, still no sign of a delivery.

"Boy, I'm gonna fuck Marlon over good if this tip doesn't pan out," he said out loud.

"Where is that shit anyway?" Tramell asked.

"I don't know. I haven't seen him for two days now." Redding answered.

A crackle was now heard coming from Redding's radio. Suddenly, Detective Simmons' voice came through.

"Heads up people. Red Beamer coming up the block. License plate FRANK, GARY, APPLE, 3-4-9. You'll hear them."

"Yes, motherfucker. That's them!" Redding yelled as he was pumped up and full of energy now. Trammell let out one last big breath. He could feel the adrenaline racing through his body.

"We're going to 10-3 for precautionary measures until further notice," another voice was heard, this one coming from Lieutenant Horowitz.

"He thinks they're listening in?" Trammell asked as he looked over at Redding.

"Marlon said they've been using scanners in the PJ's. We can't take any chances," Redding replied.

"That's fucking ridiculous," Trammell said disgusted.

"Yeah well, if you want to point fingers — how about blaming businesses like Radio Shack for that?" Redding said.

A slight bass thump could be heard in the distance as the detectives sat back in their seats. Redding looked at his side mirror and finally saw the vehicle turning the corner. It was a red 1989 BMW, 535i Series. It had tinted windows all around and some fancy chromed out rims. The music blasting from the car was insane as it passed them. Tramell could feel the vibrations from the music in his chest. It was either the rap song playing or his heart thumping profusely.

The Beamer eventually parked on the corner of the block, and Jordan stepped out of the vehicle. He was accompanied by another black male, a huge brooding individual that stood about 6'10, known in the hood as Beazel. They both crossed the street and headed for the bodega. Meanwhile, Redding and Tramell looked on quizzically.

"I don't know, but for a delivery these guys are sure traveling light," Tramell said.

"Shit. I was just thinking the same damn thing," Redding added.

Jordan entered the store followed by his partner. A Dominican male behind the counter greeted them as they walked in; the man went by Diego.

"¿negro de mierda, que pasa?" He spoke to them in Spanish, making sure to raise his voice as he asked what's up by calling Jordan a black piece of shit.

"Fuck you too, Diego," Jordan answered back, playfully sticking out his middle finger for good measure.

"Where is everybody?" Beazel spoke.

"They're all downstairs, they waiting for you," Diego replied with a heavy accent.

The two gentlemen proceeded towards the back of the store, making a slight right near the pet food section. Behind a beaded curtain was a set of narrow stairs leading to the basement. As they made their way down, the sounds of the wooden steps creaked and squeaked. More so by the weight of Beazel, who also ducked as he went down, trying to avoid knocking his head.

The basement was dingy looking and musky smelling, the effects of an apparent leak as the ground was wet. Both gentlemen simultaneously tiptoed, desperately attempting not to ruin the expensive sneakers they wore. Jordan was furious.

"Man, this is bullshit!" He barked.

"It's just water, my friends." They heard a voice in the distance.

They continued further, arriving at an open door. Inside the small room were three men. One of which held a cane in front of him while he sat. His name was Martine Rosa.

He was in his late fifties with crisp solid white hair. His two hulking sons, Gabriel and Frankie, were at his side.

Martine was of Dominican nationality, born in San Pedro de Macoris. He'd been an official U.S. citizen for some time, making the most of the American dream. Along with his two sons, they had accomplished owning three bodegas, one in Queens, the Bronx, and this one in Brooklyn.

Apart from selling groceries, the Rosa family surrounded themselves in wealth by illegal ventures. Their main choice of extra income involved selling cocaine and marijuana. Certain individuals would be able to buy it right out of their stores, as long as they were known buyers or used passwords that frequently changed, in order to throw off any prying enforcement types.

"You guys need to do something about this water shit down here," Jordan continued nagging.

"Esto negros le importan la ropa mas que nada," Martine whispered, smiling at his racism in telling his men that the two cared more for their clothes than anything else. It was loud enough to get a laugh from his two sons behind him.

"English motherfucker, English," Jordan retaliated.

Martine and Jordan shook hands as he took a seat opposite the older gentleman. The meeting was about to begin.

"I have done good business with you for several years. But this is what it comes down to? It's been three weeks." Martine said.

"And you know how Tre feels about all of this. If it's gonna happen then let it. We've been doing just fine despite everything being switched up," Jordan said.

••••••••••

Meanwhile, the two detectives stared intently at the store. They were hoping to see Lamont and his friend step out so that they could swoop in and arrest them.

At this moment, a young Hispanic looking woman crossed the street with a little boy, about the age of six. They were heading straight to the store. The woman wore a black colored raincoat with a large brown shoulder bag. Both detectives saw her and the boy and reacted miserably.

"Aw fuck! She's going in. Stay home lady, will ya," Redding yelled.

"It's too late now. Let's just hope nothing goes down until she leaves," Tramell added.

"Unit 12, do something to prevent anyone else from going in that store. Do you copy?" Horowitz's voice boomed over the CB.

"Roger that," Tramell said as he spoke into his radio.

"Fuck! This is fucked right now!" Redding yelled.

"I'll go… I'll cross the street and stand in that doorway," Tramell said.

"That's real nice. You're gonna be like the only white asshole in this neighborhood standing around nonchalantly late at night," Redding said unhappily.

Tramell slowly got out of the vehicle and looked around. He was trying really hard not to look suspicious as he crossed the street. At best, he was gunning for someone to mistake him for some crackhead looking for a seller.

He made it to a building doorway three stores down from the bodega and waited. Surprisingly, the block was pretty quiet except for a few passing cars from time to time. He now glanced over at Redding in the car. Tramell then motioned towards the bodega with his head. Redding signaled back by shaking his head no. For now, things were at a standstill.

••••••••••

Martine held on to the wooden, hand carved top of his cane with a firm grip.

"How well do you trust this young fellow of yours?" He asked Jordan.

"According to Tre, he's supposed to be reliable," Jordan responded.

"I didn't ask about Tre. I asked how do *you* feel about Marlon?" Martine answered back.

"I don't have a problem with him. But, then again, I'm not the one in charge," Jordan said as he looked at the elder gentleman.

A sudden eerie silence fell in the room. Martine finally held onto his cane with both hands as he attempted to stand. He was immediately helped by his son Gabriel. Jordan took this as a sign to also stand up. The two men looked at each other. Martine then extended his hand out and they both shook hands.

"I'll meet with one of your sons tomorrow," Jordan said.

Martine just shook his head and agreed. Jordan and Beazel now turned around and headed out the door.

As they walked out, Martine kept a firm eye on the two then finally headed back upstairs.

....

Tramell continued to wait in the doorway. He frequently checked with Redding for any movement from the store. Suddenly, he heard a bell sound. It came from the door to the bodega being opened. It was the woman and her boy.

They made their way out with bags in hand. The woman carried two, while her son carried the other. They passed the doorway as the woman looked over to the side and saw Tramell standing there. She was instantly startled as she nudged her child to move faster. Tramell continued looking at this woman as if something were out of place, but he just couldn't pinpoint anything at this particular moment. He watched the woman as she reached the end of the block and began to cross the street.

Tramell would eventually shrug it off as he looked back at the car. He saw that Redding was holding out his hand in a stop motion as he looked on at the bodega like a hawk.

Finally, he saw both Jordan and Beazel approaching the door. Redding quickly snatched his radio.

"This is unit 12, everyone in position," he said.

Tramell heard the bell sound once again. He proceeded to stick his head out just enough to see the two men starting to cross the street as they joked around with each other. Tramell looked back at Redding who had begun a countdown with his fingers. Four. Three. Two. Finally, one. He then signaled for Tramell to make his move.

As the gentlemen reached their vehicle, a frantic display of police cars and detectives emerged onto the street from all angles. Tramell raced up behind the two men with his gun drawn.

"Get on your fucking knees right now!" He yelled.

Detectives were already rushing into the bodega with guns out. The block had quickly become a dizzying array of red and blue lights bouncing off the building walls. Redding had sped up, stopping his car in back of the Beamer. He bolted out of the vehicle and headed straight to Jordan, pressing his knee into his back as both men were on the ground. Strangely, Jordan appeared calm throughout the chaotic scene unfolding.

"May I ask what the hell is going on?" Jordan spoke.

"Shut the fuck up you piece of shit!" He was quickly greeted with a response by Redding.

Both gentlemen were now being cuffed and searched from shoulder to ankle. Redding took care of his man while detective Ronald Simmons, took care of Beazel. Simmons was a big husky black man with forearms that resembled that of Popeye's. He made sure Beazel felt them as he pressed on the back of his neck.

"Nothing, huh," Simmons said.

"You fucking assholes got nothing on us," Beazel yelled.

"Shut your mouth!" Simmons barked as he pressed down on Beazel's cheek.

Beazel's head found itself swiftly sandwiched between a heavy forearm and cold concrete.

Lieutenant Horowitz made his way across the street. He was a muscular looking man who stood about 6'6. The inside joke with many detectives was about his thick brown mustache, which resembled that of a seventies porn star. Horowitz didn't look so thrilled behind that mustache for the current situation.

"The big bust so far is turning out to be a big nothing," he said.

The detectives were at a loss for words. Tramell would take on and off again peeks down the block, faintly still eyeing the woman and her child. There was that weird feeling again. He noticed that the woman had stopped and was looking at the commotion going down. Tramell looked back over at Jordan and Beazel on the ground. Something just kept bothering him about the whole situation. As the two men were being lifted, it finally hit him.

Tramell quickly turned and faced Horowitz, he looked at him with a wild look in his eyes.

"Son of a bitch! They made the fucking deal!" He yelled.

"What the hell are you talking about?" Horowitz insisted.

"The woman who left the store, she had a brown bag when she entered. Son of a bitch!" Tramell said as he looked back down the block, trying not to lose sight of the woman.

Redding now thought of it.

"He's right. She wasn't carrying the bag when she left," Redding chimed in.

"Dammit!" Tramell screamed as he turned and began to run down the block as fast as he could.

Meanwhile, Jordan's calm demeanor had slowly begun to fade. Tramell's bag theory had definitely struck a nerve. Tramell began to run, noticing the woman had turned around and had begun to walk quicker, an occasional push on the back of her son to move along.

Tramell had completed numerous trainings leading up to this sting, physical exercises that exerted every last bit of wind in his lungs. The moment he now faced, it was all surreal to realize his own stamina. He knew he was running top speed, but it felt like it took forever to reach this woman. He could see that she was halfway to another block constantly looking back at him it seemed.

Redding had gotten back into his car and slammed his door. His tires skidded leaving the smell of rubber in the air and track marks on the street from a massive U-turn.

Tramell had almost caught up to the woman. As he got closer, he could make out the nervous look on her face as he continued giving chase.

Suddenly, a black Lincoln Town car pulled up towards the corner. The woman quickly opened the door and practically threw her son in the back seat along with the bags they held. She then jumped in the back and closed the door.

"Stop!" Tramell yelled as he was half way there now.

It didn't help. The red break lights in the back of the car turned off. He knew it was about to pull away. As the car began moving, a huge monkey wrench was about to be thrown into the mix.

Tramell was out of breath, when a black colored car raced up the opposite side of the block and turned towards the Lincoln, blocking it.

Two gentleman wearing ski masks jumped out of the vehicle. One had a huge sawed off shotgun, the other a nine-millimeter handgun.

Tramell had stopped dead in his tracks. He was dumbfounded at what he was now witnessing. The man with the shotgun stepped up to the car and aimed his gun at the windshield. Without saying a word, he fired. There was a loud bang accompanied by a flashing light. The bullet spray had shattered the windshield to pieces along with the drivers face.

Tramell could hear the woman and her child screaming hysterically from the back seat.

"This is detective Tramell, I need back-up. Shots fired! I repeat shots fired. New Lots Avenue and Bradford," he yelled into his radio.

Tramell immediately drew his gun as he ducked near a parked car. He could hear Redding's car in the distance fast approaching.

The sawed-off gunman now reached into the car taking out the bags which he took back to the other vehicle. As he got in, the other gunman ran to the back of the Town Car.

The woman screamed and yelled, pleading for her life. The gunman reached into the car and grabbed her by the hair, pulling her out of the vehicle. He viciously threw the woman on the ground and aimed his pistol at her. He then pumped four shots into the woman as her son watched in horror from the back seat.

Tramell desperately inched his way closer to the scene. He was only three cars away.

"Come on! Get the fuck in the car!" He heard the driver yell, but business wasn't finished. The other gunman aimed his pistol in the back seat, right at the screaming boy.

Trammell had to make his move. He finally leaped out from his hiding spot and quickly fired three shots, hitting the gunman in his chest. As his body hit the ground, the mysterious black car fishtailed off. Tramell tried running behind it, getting close enough to fire one shot that broke through the back window. The bullet pierced the driver's right arm as he yelled in pain but sped off nonetheless.

Tramell attempted to get a license plate number, but it was too late as the car turned a corner.

"Fuck!" Tramell screamed.

He was pissed off at everything that had gone down. He was way beyond training. The reality of his new job was sinking in — evident by the three dead bodies he was looking at and the uncontrollable screaming and crying from the boy in the back seat of the Town Car.

Chapter 7

"Chester and the Start of Something Really Bad"

Drugs are a sickness. It doesn't matter which side of the spectrum you're on. If you use, you want more and more. If you sell, you need more to sell in order to make more money. I was liking the idea of selling. I had found something I was pretty good at. My math skills in school even improved. Other than that, Abraham was helping me get by academically. I wouldn't say I was dumb, it was just that my attention span was small and it was all focused on the color green. Green for the weed and green for the money.

I had approached Rolando about needing more product. I started bagging and selling dimes and twenties. The middle school kids didn't hold that kind

of bank. So, I turned to Rosemary for help. She let her

brother know about the stuff and just like that,

another outlet was opened up. Rolando used to warn

me. He'd say, while making money was fun, there

would come a time where I was going to be tested.

That if things were going great, there was always

going to be someone out to burst your bubble. He

asked me how far I would really go to prove myself

in those situations.

I was considered a drug dealer. My mother was

dying. My brother was handicapped. Any sympathy

my heart felt slowly faded with each year I grew

older. How far do you think I went?

···········

It was October 14th, 1989. This particular Saturday morning was a dreary one. It had been pouring outside and the forecast for the rest of the day was a lot of the same. I hung out in my room all day along with Taz, Duckie, Abraham, and Jose. We all listened to music and joked around, enjoying some pastelitos de guayaba that Duckie had brought over. He always had the best guava pastries.

Race or color had nothing to do with food when it came to Duckie, he enjoyed all kinds. His favorite though, was starting to be Spanish food. On his way to my building, Duckie would always stop by a Puerto Rican owned restaurant on Jerome Avenue. It was known as the best cuchifrito spot on the strip. You could get any fried food you could think of there. He would sometimes buy arroz con gandules because rice with pigeon beans was one of his top five. Mostly he copped another one of his favorites though, the fried tube shaped snack made out of green plantains and filled with ground beef called an alcapurria, although Duckie could never pronounce the word. He would always point at the things and ask for a certain amount. The gringo was cute according to the waitresses that worked there; they always served him quickly and with a smile.

The four of us made the most of the ugly day. We talked about music, clothes, bitches, money, and weed. The latter, taking up the most time. As soon as the drug lingo began to take over, Abraham went back to what he had originally come to my crib to do. He was putting the final touches on a report of China that was due in my social studies class. He was also getting paid twenty dollars for it.

"I need a cigarette," Duckie complained as he reached into his pocket, taking out a pack of Newport cigarettes.

"Not in here man. You want to smoke, take that shit outside bro," I responded.

Duckie didn't seem too thrilled at the idea as he slowly got up while moaning. He looked over at Taz and asked him if he wanted to join. Taz agreed. As they reached the front door I could hear Rolando grilling them out of nowhere.

"Where you guys going?" Rolando asked sternly.

"Outside for a minute," Duckie answered.

Rolando knew exactly where they were going and bitched some more about it by adding, "I know. You better not toss your butts in front of that dumb bitch's door."

Duckie told me later how they had quickly left the apartment cutting off any hint of an extended conversation with Rolando. For starters, they feared the man. Secondly, any time Rolando would spend in the hospital with Mildred, he would come home extra stressed out and agitated. Rolando had apparently walked Mildred into the living room in this instance, where she sat on the couch. The rapid progression of her disease was causing all kinds of complications now.

The latest was something called Pneumocystis Carinii Pneumonia (PCP). Mildred's monthly doctor appointment consisted of her having to inhale the drug Pentamidine through a nebulizer. The side effects were the worst. She often felt nauseous for hours after the treatment. Rolando would let her stay on the couch because the trips to the bathroom to vomit were shorter than if she were lying down on her bed. He would also leave a little bucket by the side of the couch for good measure, just in case she fell asleep and couldn't get up at all.

Ever since her diagnosis with AIDS, Rolando had shown a different side. He was more empathetic with Mildred. Welfare was paying for her doctor visits, but many drugs that were coming out around this time were still in clinical trial runs. Rolando would often have to come out of his pocket to pay for them and they weren't cheap by any means.

Between the Pentamidine for her pneumonia and Zidovudine (AZT) for the AIDS, Mildred was racking up a large monthly bill. My grandmother constantly argued with Mildred on the days she was feeling somewhat alright. She never cared for Rolando and likened everything they were going through as a punishment from God. She would tell her daughter that it was kind of sad, that after Rolando used to give her drugs for free in order for her to get high, he was now paying for other drugs to try and make her get better.

Mildred lay down on the couch and closed her eyes while Rolando went into the kitchen. He'd opened the refrigerator and grabbed himself a can of beer. It was still morning time, but Rolando's day had felt like an eternity he told me.

"Antonio!" he yelled. I could hear his annoying voice from my bedroom. I groaned but had no other choice than to stroll into the kitchen and attend to him.

"Yeah, papi. What's up?" I answered nonchalantly.

"What are you guys up to?" Rolando asked, all the while observing me closely.

"Nothing. We're just hanging out," I replied.

"Well, that nothing you mentioned just went out into the hall to smoke a cigarette. I'm not stupid. You know that fucking bitch Consuela made another complaint about smelling smoke, right? I should go over there right now and piss on her door," Rolando vented. He then took another swig of his beer, finishing it.

Rolando was referring to the old lady that lived next to our apartment. She was one of those nosy types who constantly had her eye and ears to the door whenever any movement was heard in the hallway. Rolando always feared the fact that enough complaints by her to management would result in extra attention to the apartment. It was hard enough keeping everything looking right for the ACS worker several years ago. The last thing he wanted was someone else paying them a visit and doing regular check-ups. His real cause for concern stemmed from the fact that Rolando would frequently bring over large bundles of product and leave it in the apartment along with cash.

"Alright. I'll tell Duckie," I told him.

"Hey, how's everything going?" He then asked me.

"Good. I called my homegirl up. Her brother goes to Clinton. He's gonna try and hook me up with some of his friends," I answered.

"Just be careful. I have some good stuff coming in on Tuesday, so I'll let you know. Now get out of here," Rolando said.

I exited the kitchen with my head down. Apart from hearing about some new weed coming in and the potential to keep making money, my upbeat attitude would always change whenever my mother and Rolando returned from the hospital. It was out of embarrassment that I felt this way. I knew my friends knew about my mother and the whole AIDS thing, even though they never spoke about it. The fact that she was now plopped on the couch for the whole world to see was making me feel even more uncomfortable.

At that moment, Duckie and Taz walked back into the apartment, leaving the front door semi-opened.

"Ant, your uncle is outside with some guy. They want to speak with Ro," Duckie said.

"Let them come in," I answered him.

My Uncle Chester now walked into the apartment with a black duffel bag over his left shoulder, followed by a black gentleman. Chester was in his late

thirties and always sported a thick beard. This was to

hide a fat scar that ran from one side of his right ear,

along his cheek and right underneath his chin. It was

a constant reminder of a blatant attempt to try and

kill him during a stint at the Elmira Correctional

Facility in Chemung County, New York, he explained

to me one day.

"Damn Antonio! You're getting big and shit. How

are you bro?" Chester asked.

"I'm okay, *tío*," I responded, very blasé.

"Yo, check it. Where's Rolando? I wanted to speak

with him about something," Chester asked.

"He's in the kitchen," I said.

"Hey Ant, this here is my boy, Marlon," Chester

then told me as he pointed towards his mystery

friend who was halfway in the apartment now.

I instantly looked at Marlon, nodding my head as I acknowledged him. Marlon looked back at me approvingly.

"Alright little brother. What's happening?" Marlon said to me. This Marlon guy was a strange looking individual. He was lanky and dirty looking. He reeked of cigarettes and had two missing teeth. All of this had been observed by me in a matter of seconds while I continued to look at him up and down. *Notch this encounter as adding yet another person to the dysfunctional atmosphere that inhabited my world,* I thought.

Chester slowly inched further into the apartment and poked his head into the living room. He immediately saw Mildred asleep on the couch. He walked in and knelt in front of her just staring. He

then leaned in and gave his sister a kiss on the
forehead. Chester knew that his sister was suffering
immensely and any day her illness could take a turn
for the worst. Chester was making it a habit of
visiting more often because of it. There had been a
long stretch of time in both of their lives where the
two had gone their separate ways. While Mildred
turned to drugs for her escapism, Chester was out
making a name for himself on the streets I'd heard.

It varied depending on the gravity of the situation
he was in. If Chester needed money, there was always
a different means he'd go about to obtain cash. He
would sell drugs, or simply wait for some
unsuspecting person to step off the train at Hunts
Point. Acts of these kind were the reason for his
extended rap sheet with local authorities. The list also
included drug use, gun possession, gun selling, and

gang activity. Chester made it a habit of living his life in and out of jail, with a year and six months being his longest stay in one... so far.

Supposedly, he and a few of his friends found the need to seek retribution on a rival drug dealer by the name of Manny "El Flaco" Colon. Chester and crew always loved the club scene, frequenting a parade of spots on weekends. One club in particular was called the "Devil's Nest" located on Webster and Tremont Avenues in the Bronx — way before my time. The guys supposedly had pull with many of the bouncers that worked there, always getting in without fully being frisked. The lack of proper security procedures enabled them to smuggle in drugs hidden inside cigarette boxes along with small blades under the in-soles of their shoes or sneakers. Chester even showed me how he did it once.

One Saturday night, they were told of a guy named Manny visiting the club in order to catch a performance of this group called the "Cover Girls". It wasn't for any other reason but to show up another dealer that Chester would eventually find himself in the bathroom alone with — Manny. He proceeded to stab him in the back using a three-inch blade tactical knife as he pissed in the urinal, Chester explained. He then stomped and kicked him several times cracking two ribs. The most damage of this humiliating and severe beat down was directed at Manny's face. The steel tipped boots Chester wore made direct contact, breaking his jaw and knocking out a pretty good amount of his teeth.

A woman hanging out with Manny that night would eventually ID Chester as the only other person in the bathroom at the time. The beat down along with other infractions had violated his parole and Chester was forced to do time.

In prison, all it takes is one person to get ahold of another person that knows someone else locked up with somebody and a full-blown revenge plot can be put in motion. In this instance, Manny had sent a kite to a cousin of his doing some time in Elmira. The end result of the letter was an inmate running up on Chester and slicing his face, scarring him for life. Manny had originally called for someone to "body" Chester. He wanted him dead. But Chester defended himself valiantly, he said. Despite his effort though, he was still given a "buck fifty" instead. That was in reference to the slice on his face, so opened up that it would take one hundred and fifty stitches or better to close. In Chester's case, it took a hundred and seventy-eight.

I saw Chester and Marlon continuing towards the kitchen. My curiosity was always at full peak, especially when it came down to Rolando's kind of business. The fact that my uncle and his new-found friend had walked into the apartment with a duffel bag only meant this was one of "those" meetings. *Maybe the stuff that was supposedly coming in on Tuesday had found its way into Chester's hand a couple of days early?* This is what I had originally thought.

Chester looked in the kitchen while knocking on the hallway wall.

"Rolando," he whispered.

"What's up?" I heard Rolando say.

Chester then eased into the kitchen, probably slapped Rolando five or something. Meanwhile, Marlon stood in the hallway just waiting. Rolando had noticed him immediately when I heard him yell out, "Who the fuck is that?"

"Ro, that's my friend Marlon, he's cool man, believe me." I heard Chester say trying to ease the tension.

"What's going on man?" Rolando asked, all the while maintaining focus on the strange gentleman halfway in his kitchen. Apparently, the look on Rolando's face was that of being very pissed off.

Continuing to try and move things along, Chester had quickly thrown the duffel bag on the kitchen table. "I need to show you something, Rolando," Chester said excitedly.

"What is it now, another one of your get rich quick schemes or what?" Rolando yelled out.

"Nah man. It's better than that," Chester said.

Rolando seemed intrigued at the thought of something new. He was always opened to at least hearing Chester out whenever he presented him with some sort of new venture. Rolando stared at the duffel bag but would also take frequent peeks at the strange gentleman somewhat in his kitchen. Until he finally couldn't take it anymore.

"Chester, do me a favor. Tell him to come inside the kitchen," I could hear Rolando say.

Without Chester even saying a word, Marlon had obliged Ro's wishes, quickly walking in without saying a word.

"Now, what the fuck is this?" Rolando asked.

"Just open it, Ro," Chester said.

Rolando zipped open the bag and looked inside. His eyes instantly widened I could imagine. Inside the duffel bag were six bricks of cocaine wrapped up in cellophane.

"Where the fuck did you get this?" Rolando demanded.

"We made a little move," Chester answered.

"What kind of fucking move did you make?" Rolando asked defensively.

There was a brief moment of silence in the kitchen after that I remember.

"Well, are you going to answer me or what?" Rolando then barked out.

"We kind of knocked somebody," Chester said.

"Are you out of your mind!? ¿Tu estas loco?" Rolando screamed as he jumped out of his chair. I could hear it drag across the kitchen floor.

"It's nothing man. I figured you're the man to talk to about possibly making some money with this," Chester pleaded his case.

Whatever stress Rolando had been feeling, it had been instantly doubled once Chester entered the kitchen with the bag full of cocaine. I could hear a lot of movement coming from the kitchen. It was probably Rolando pacing back and forth like he often did whenever confronted with a dilemma.

"Who did you knock for this? Was it big Donovan from Castle Hill?" Rolando screamed out.

"No! It's some guys from Brooklyn. You don't know them," Chester explained.

"This is crazy man. This is fucking crazy right now," Rolando rambled.

I heard the refrigerator door open, Rolando had grabbed yet another beer. I heard the can open up as he must have gulped half of it down.

"How are you involved with this shit?" Rolando then asked Marlon. I know Marlon was scared, I could hear it in his voice when he answered back.

"I put my boy Chester onto these cats. I knew they were holding some good stuff. They were selling it out of their crib, so we planned it out and robbed the place, and… here it is," Marlon explained.

And there it was indeed. Pure white, uncut cocaine. It were very beautiful to say the least. But it still meant problems.

"Chester, this isn't good, man," Rolando said.

"Why not? I know you can move it, Ro," Chester answered.

"Chester, you're not getting the picture. This shit isn't just an ounce of weed. This is some heavy business you have right here. I don't care who you robbed for it but, this white is definitely being missed by someone right now," Rolando said.

"Hey Chester, let's just get out of here," Marlon interrupted.

"Shut the fuck up! Both of you have some nerve coming into my house with this amount of yay-yo and act like it's all cool!" Rolando now screamed.

Chester quickly got in between Rolando and Marlon. He knew that much of his anger right now had more to do with Marlon being a stranger in his apartment.

"Easy man, relax, Rolando," Chester said.

Back in my room, the muffled sounds of arguing continued coming from the kitchen. I had walked away at one point, but the drama unfolding still had me intrigued. I had even asked Jose to turn down the radio that was playing.

"Yo Ant, what's going on?" Duckie asked.

"I don't know. But, I have to get closer," I said as I walked out of my room and headed towards the kitchen.

I stuck my head out first just in case the meeting had been finished. By the sound of the continued bickering going on, the three men were still in the kitchen. I now quietly crept with my back against the wall, making my way closer to the kitchen. As I passed the living room, I had glanced over at my mother on the couch. I had taken a whiff of the air and quickly covered my nose and mouth. It was the smell of vomit that had entered my nasal passages causing a gag reflex. Mildred's throw-up was all over the carpet and beginning to stink up the apartment. She obviously never made it to the bathroom, nor did Rolando ever get the bucket for her. He was too preoccupied at the moment with Chester, Marlon and six bricks of cocaine on the kitchen table.

Rolando had calmed down dramatically it seemed. In fact, the tone of everyone's voice had settled.

"So, what are you guys looking to get for this?" Rolando asked.

"A hundred," I heard Chester reply.

"That's not going to happen," Rolando said.

"No way! You're looking at about sixteen plus, Rolando," Chester explained.

"Ten each, maybe eleven." Rolando countered.

"Nah man. There has to be someone willing to go at least thirteen to fourteen," Chester argued.

"It's not happening Chester. There's too much involved."

"What about twelve then?" Chester asked.

"Maybe, but it's not guaranteed. You have to understand that, first of all, someone is going to be hesitant about this quantity coming from out of nowhere. Me, personally, I have to know for sure that it's some good stuff. If it is, it will sell quicker. But, it all depends on whether or not there are eyes on this." Rolando said.

"I'm telling you Ro, it was just some punks trying to step up their game, that's it," Chester said.

"There was nothing else, no money? You're gonna tell me that these punks just had six bricks lying around but no cash?" Rolando grilled.

I could smell the scent of cigarettes in the air. I heard both men pleading that there wasn't when Marlon had backed up a few feet and was half in the kitchen and half in the hallway. He quickly noticed me standing up against the wall just hanging out. I knew I had been found, but I remained silent, even turning my head as if not interested in the conversation going on.

"What's up? What's going on?" Rolando asked Marlon.

"Nothing. I think it's your son," Marlon answered.

"Antonio!" Rolando then screamed.

I quietly walked into the kitchen now, my head was down. I had been silently preparing myself for some kind of backlash for being nosy. It was inevitable.

"Are you looking for something?" Rolando asked me.

"No sir," I said as I continued looking down at the floor.

"So, what the fuck are you doing then?" Rolando yelled.

"Nothing. I heard arguing so I wanted to see if you needed me. You know, needed some help or something," I said, desperately trying to make whatever that had come out of my mouth sound convincing.

"You hear this kid? That's your nephew, okay. He's another knucklehead just like you," Rolando said as he looked over at Chester.

"He's alright. Right Antonio?" Chester smiled looking back at me.

Rolando took one last pull from the cigarette and threw it inside the can of beer as it fizzled. "Look, I'll see what I can do, but I'm not promising you anything. You got that?" Rolando told Chester.

Chester instantly garnered a smile from ear to ear as he looked over at his boy Marlon. The strange man also smiled. Now that everyone seemed happy, I couldn't help but walk up to the table and look inside the bag. I was flabbergasted.

"Wow. That's a lot of fucking yay. Can I sell some of it?" I yelled out and asked.

Chester laughed at the comment as Rolando looked at me.

"*Can I sell some of it?* You hear this kid?" Rolando said.

All three gentlemen began to laugh. *I had definitely broken the ice,* I thought.

"That's my little nephew," Chester said.

He threw his hands up and playfully shadow-boxed with me. I remember him taking a swipe at me, which I ducked and then tapped Chester on the right side of his shoulder. It elicited a scream of pain from him. Rolando couldn't help but notice his reaction.

"What's wrong with you?" Rolando asked.

"Nothing. I've been working out so I'm still a little sore, that's all," Chester answered immediately, still trying to maintain a smile on his face.

••••••••••

[N.Y.P.D., 75th PRECINCT]

Rain drops rapidly tapped against the window glass as Lamont Jordan sat in a chair. He looked up at the small sized window with steel bars running down

it. He always marveled at the fact that many precincts

and jails would strategically place a window in a

holding cell or interrogating room. It was the one

glimpse of hope for any detainee, that if they

cooperated with police or detectives, they could soon

be on the opposite side of the wall and back on the

streets.

He'd been sitting in this confined room now for

twenty minutes and no one had entered. Yet another

mind game played by the cops to see what he would

do, or was doing. Lamont knew very well that he was

being watched on the other side of the mirror he

frequently checked himself in.

Detectives Tramell and Redding looked through the

double-sided mirror, observing Lamont. They

watched as he got out of his seat and walked closer to the mirror. He then began to pick at something on his cheek.

"A face only a mother could love, huh? I feel like going in there right now and fucking cracking him one," Redding joked.

At this time, Lieutenant Horowitz and detective Simmons entered the room.

"What's up fellas, anything going on with Jordan?" Horowitz asked.

"Nothing. We haven't gone in yet," Tramell replied.

Horowitz then handed Tramell a folder which he took a peek at. Inside was a series of photos of the shooting victims from the night before.

"Show him those, see what his reaction is,"
Horowitz said.

Tramell nodded as he and Redding exited the
room.

The door to the interrogating room opened as
Tramell and Redding walked inside.

"Sit the fuck down in the chair, Lamont," Redding
ordered.

"Yeah, yeah. I'm moving, relax," Lamont said as he
did what he was told.

The detectives took a seat opposite Lamont as they
looked at him.

"So, are you going to tell us something or what?"
Tramell questioned. Lamont simply rolled his eyes.

"Look, I already told you. I don't know what you
guys are talking about, so do what you want with that

statement," Lamont answered rolling his eyes again at the cops.

It was in the manner that he spoke, with such cockiness and certainty that had Redding wanting to reach over the desk and pop Jordan in the face.

"Listen you little shit, believe me when I tell you that we can make your life miserable, you hear me?" Redding lashed out at Jordan.

"I could care less what you say, or how threateningly you say it. Either charge me with something or let me go. I have rights you know. As a matter of fact, I want to petition a writ of habeas corpus."

"You know what Jordan? You can take your habeas corpus and shove it in your ass," Tramell said.

Horowitz and Simmons watched and listened to the interrogation from the opposite side of the room. As of that moment, Jordan wasn't giving up any information.

Suddenly, the door opened and detective Carlos Acevedo walked in. He was another undercover assigned to the narcotics division. Acevedo often worked in the predominantly Hispanic areas of Brooklyn because of his ability to speak fluent Spanglish.

"I have some info on your guy Marlon," he told Horowitz as he handed him a paper.

"What is it?" Horowitz said.

"Take a look at it."

Horowitz scanned the paper then looked back at the two detectives in the other room.

"Call them in here please," he asked Simmons.

"Tramell, Redding, can you come into the room for a minute?" Simmons said, his finger pressing on a button on the wall.

Jordan heard Simmons' voice and looked at the two detectives with a snug type smile.

"Peace out brothers," he said.

Tramell just looked at him and then leaned in closer.

"I know that you know something. But, it's cool. Keep playing your role. We're gonna continue to dig until we have so much dirt on you, not even the best lawyer you can find will want to consult with your ass. I promise you. Every street you walk on, every corner you turn, we're gonna be there waiting for you. I'm gonna follow you like a shadow, like some fucking ghost, man," he told Jordan.

"You go right ahead and do that, you big ole' Casper looking motherfucker," Jordan replied.

The detectives now stood up from their seats as Tramell took one last attempt at something. He proceeded to flick the folder in his hand towards Jordan.

"I want you to look at the pictures in that folder. I know you don't give a fuck, but just look at them anyway. That woman that left the store right before you and your boy came out, was gunned down right in front of her son. The driver of the car she was getting into was also killed. Forensics probably had a field day with that one because his head and brain were all over the back seat. Look at those photos, maybe it'll refresh your memory or spark something in that stupid head of yours. Maybe you can remember what was in the bags she was carrying, which were stolen by the way," Tramell said as he turned around and headed for the door.

The three detectives on the other side continued watching Jordan. He seemed to be a bit unsettled as he slowly opened the folder and looked at the pictures inside.

At this moment, Redding and Tramell entered the room.

"Jordan looks a bit ruffled," Simmons said.

"Yeah well, fuck him for now," Redding answered.

"Carlos has some news about your man Marlon," Horowitz told the detectives.

"Word on the streets of Brooklyn is that Marlon is a dead man walking. Nobody is saying who wants him clipped, but, I think we can figure that one out for ourselves," Acevedo explained.

"NLT. They caught on to him blabbing to us," Tramell said.

"Problem is the entire store was clean other than the woman's bag which was found in a dumpster out back. The fact remains we still have no solid evidence against Jordan and Beazel or the Rosa family. It also means that Marlon's tips didn't help us out at all," Acevedo replied.

The room was silent as Tramell walked over to the mirror and took a peek at Jordan. As he watched him, Tramell was deep in thought. He then turned around and looked at Horowitz.

"I have a theory," he said to him.

"Shoot it rook," Horowitz replied.

"Redding said that Marlon used to run with NLT. He basically was given a lesser role once Jordan stepped into the picture. Therefore, he wasn't making as much money. My question is this, what if Marlon dicked both NLT and us?" Tramell said.

"What are you getting at?" Horowitz questioned.

"It had to be more than a coincidence that we raid these guys last night and they still pull off a deal the way they did. You don't just change a routine from one day to the next. On any normal day, these Rosa stores are supposedly hot. Anyone can walk in and buy chips, a quarter juice and a bag of blow. All of a sudden these guys and that one store are squeaky clean? Let's just say they may have been conducting business a little differently, waiting to get hit up. Marlon uses us to cause a distraction knowing that he or whomever can catch up with the woman a couple of blocks down and snatch the product," Tramell said, his theory definitely getting the attention of everyone in the room.

"Okay, I admit it sounds like a stretch, but a viable one at that. If it is valid, this only means we need to find that rat before NLT does. If not, we still have nothing," Horowitz said.

Redding now walked over to the mirror and looked at Jordan in the other room. Jordan was fast asleep with his head leaning back and his mouth wide open.

"So much for sparking Jordan's memory. There goes your fucking New Lots terror, knocked the fuck out," Redding said as he shook his head in disbelief.

Chapter 8

"Going Down"

It was towards Christmas that year of 1989 that I had two steady weed spots that were doing good business. Rosemary's brother Pedro, turned out to be a vital asset to have. He put me onto many of his brothers and sisters by way of the gang he was in and they bought from me with regularity. Apart from them, I had become friends with many of the high schoolers that Pedro knew, and they bought weed also. I was finally looking at a decent amount of money in profit. There was nothing that could stop this train that was called the Foo Crew. We had both our middle school and Clinton High School on lock down.

While other dealers took care of cocaine or crack, the Foo were known as the weed guys. But like any success story, there was also some drama involved. One thing that becomes a part of you when you deal a drug is the paranoia. I thought it was just Rolando when I used to watch him do his thing. But, it's everybody. You constantly have to look over your shoulder, make sure no one is watching. You have to gain trust in the person you're dealing to, make sure they aren't trying to set you up to the police or even trying to rob you. Fuck, I nearly shit in my pants one day when I was approached by a gym teacher.

My class was over and I had gone to the lockers to change. He came up to me and told me he knew what I did. The dead silence after his words was enough to give anybody a fucking heart attack. He then asked to buy forty dollars' worth. Wasn't that a bitch?

The other drama involved was what Rolando spoke about often. The rivals. The other cats in the world of dealing that test you. We had to take care of that situation in an entirely different manner.

··········

Every day, I found myself going over the same routine. I'd sit in my English class and constantly look at my watch. I would then look over at the clock on the wall and compare the time on my wrist. The clock on the wall was five minutes slower and yet I chose to torture myself day in and day out just waiting for the bell to sound.

Once it did, I would quickly gather all my belongings and scamper out of the classroom ahead of everyone else. A couple of years ago it was because of my love for an animated television show that I'd race home. But things were different now. I had a business that I was in charge of. While I trusted my friends and the work they did for me, I still wanted to always have my hand in the mix. This was one of the reasons why I rarely chose to cut out from school. The mentality was that if I wasn't there in class one day, the need to get high would bring my regular buyers to someone else. On that level, I had fully embodied Rolando's teachings. He was making money, but there was always room to make more.

I hurried along one day side stepping the oncoming rush of students that scrambled for the exits. I would always make my way towards a back exit leading into the schoolyard. By cutting across the yard I eliminated the unnecessary headache of more students and the claustrophobic feeling of walking elbow to elbow with them on a narrow sidewalk. I also avoided having to deal with a bunch of cops and school security guards who posted up mainly at the entrance of the school.

Duckie would sometimes wait for me on a corner and the two of us would proceed to walk towards Jerome Avenue together. Lately, it was Rosemary who waited for me. The two of us had gotten closer ever since her brother decided to help me out. Pedro was even kind of liking me and wasn't as overprotective of his sister.

As I got closer towards the gate, I could see Rosemary on the corner, waiting. *She was beautiful*, I would often say to myself. Rosemary was definitely turning into quite the looker. She had silky long black hair, hazel colored eyes and a perfect smile. Not to mention, Rosemary was rapidly filling in her bra and jeans. Apart from staring at her face, I would often work my eyes down and focus on her rear-end.

I quickly ran behind Rosemary and threw my arms around her yelling, scaring her. Rosemary screamed as I leaned in and gave her a kiss on the neck. She quickly turned around and punched me on the arm as I laughed.

"You idiot, how many times have I told you not to do that? You scared the shit out of me stupid," she yelled at me. I just smiled as I continued to playfully claw at her.

Meanwhile, Rosemary found none of this amusing.

"I'm telling you Ant, I'm being serious. My mother has a heart condition and my grandmother has one too. That stuff is hereditary you know," she snapped.

"So, what are you trying to say?" I asked her.

"I'm saying that I can have one too," she said.

Her response elicited raucous laughter. I couldn't help it.

"Get the fuck out of here. You're bugging out," I then said to her.

"I scare easily Antonio, I'm not playing," she said.

We continued walking as Rosemary was silent. She seemed to still be upset at my so called childish behavior. We were cool like that. I now walked in back of her trying my best to contain the shit smile I still had on my face. I then pulled on the back part of her jacket towards her elbows.

"Quit it Ant. I'm not playing with you," she yelled as she remained ahead of me.

"Why not?" I asked her.

"'Cause I said so. Just leave me alone," Rosemary said with a mad look on her face.

"Fine, I'm sorry, okay?" I finally apologized.

"No, you're not," she answered.

"I'm sorry. I really mean it," I was sincere now as I grabbed her by the arm.

"I don't like it when you scare me, Ant. Besides, this whole situation with my brother and that guy Farib from MS is also bothering me," she told me.

Rosemary was referring to a rival gang called the MS-13's or "Mara Salvatrucha". It was a small network of teenage boys and girls mainly comprised of Salvadorans, who were slowly moving into the

Parkchester area of the Bronx. Her brother was a part of a group that bumped heads with some MS guys during a summer block party one day. One guy in particular was known as "Farib", a top lieutenant for the Parkchester set. Ever since then, both gangs had gone back and forth with idle threats towards each other with nothing really going down. I quickly brushed off her reason of fear.

"Those guys are small time and they don't have anything to do with me," I told her.

"Yeah, but you still hang out with my brother sometimes, and he told me they rolled by the school a couple of days ago. I just don't want anything happening to you, that's all," Rosemary pleaded.

I pulled her closer, wrapping my arms around her waist.

"Don't worry about it, okay? I promise you everything is going to be alright," I assured her.

I leaned in and gave her a kiss on the lips. Rosemary smiled begrudgingly as she stared back at me. She finally seemed to agree with me that everything would be hunky dory.

"Okay," she said as we continued to walk up the block.

The time was slowly approaching four thirty in the afternoon and the sky was already turning dark. Winter was in full effect as streetlights everywhere slowly flickered and finally came on. Rosemary and I made it a habit of walking to Clinton Dewitt High School every day to meet up with her brother and the rest of the crew. They would usually lounge around near the schoolyard for a while or until some guard would escort them away from the school premises.

From there the group would walk back towards the strip of Jerome Avenue and eventually separate. It was during this time that we'd discuss business with Pedro and collect any money from the rest of his friends.

This particular day the group consisted of Pedro, a girl he was messing with by the name of Vanessa, Monifa, Carl, Duckie and, Taz. The only two missing were Jose and Abraham, who only hung out on occasions because of his parent's strict attitude towards any after school activities.

The group had slowly walked from the school and ended up hanging out on some benches near the basketball courts at Jerome Park. The girls sat at one bench where they listened to music, while Duckie,

Taz, and Carl were engaged in a game of basketball. Despite the temperature being in the high thirties, the boys were quickly starting to work up a sweat as they played.

Pedro and I sat on another bench as we looked on and talked to each other.

"So, what's up with your boy?" Pedro asked.

"He should be here any minute. I spoke to him earlier. He said he was going home to pick up the stuff," I said as I flicked my wrist and looked at the time.

The basketball now rolled towards the bench as Carl walked towards us to retrieve it.

"Yo, Duckie said something about Jose stopping by the Wiz to pick up that new game he wanted for his Genesis," Carl chimed in on the conversation.

"Yeah well, my man is about to be here and I don't have any shit to give to him," Pedro complained.

I looked at my watch again. "Come on Jose. Where the fuck are you?" I remember saying to myself.

•••••••••

Jose had recanted how he quickly ran out of a "Nobody Beats the Wiz" electronic store. He was already late meeting up with the rest of us and knew for sure he would have to hear me bitch to him at one point. Who could blame him? Jose was carrying an ounce of weed in his pocket which I specifically asked him to pick up and bring down to Jerome Park. It was a pretty good one shot deal with no bagging involved that Pedro had lined up for me.

I admit, in the beginning I was kind of generous. Jose's commission on the transaction was given to him up front so he could purchase his brand-new game that he was excited to play once he got home. Jose was often reminded by all in the crew that he needed to be more on point with certain things when it came to the weed. He couldn't help it though. Video games and food overruled his judgment many times, causing me to call him "irresponsible" more often than not.

Jose quickened his stride towards the train station because he was upset, he later told me. This one time when he was being relied upon, him being late had nothing to do with the fact that he was holding a game in his hand. The bulk of time wasted was in his apartment listening to his mother give him a lecture on coming home late and making a habit of it.

Suddenly, the black Motorola beeper on his belt began to go off, he said. I could imagine Jose reaching down and finding it a bit difficult to unclip the beeper from his waist because of his stomach being in the way. When he finally looked at it, the code "911" ran across the screen repeatedly — my code, basically saying "Where the fuck are you?"

Jose said he looked down the block and noticed a pay phone on the corner. He immediately made his way towards the phone thinking of different excuses he would be able to use to explain why he still hadn't shown up at the park. This was all leading up to him being jumped by a punk named Farib and his boys.

Farib Villafuerte was eighteen years of age. He'd only been in America for three years, moving from San Salvador, El Salvador with his mother and baby sister. His mother sought the need to flee from her homeland to save her only son from the growing problem of crime and violence that was beginning to flood the streets, I'd heard. Little did she know Farib had already embraced the urban underbelly, even assisting in the killing of a thirteen-year-old boy as part of a gang initiation.

The word "Mara" was tattooed in black scripted letters across the knuckles on his right hand as he gripped the steering wheel of a 1986 burgundy colored Oldsmobile. Along for the ride was Ceasar, riding shotgun, with Dusty and Carlos in the backseat I assumed. The four teens just drove around the neighborhood bopping their heads to the music blaring from the speakers. This was normal for them.

As the car slowly rode by, Ceasar must have caught Jose's eye walking towards the corner. He probably noticed him more so for the black and yellow colored bandana that hung out of Jose's back pocket. Although Jose wasn't a part of the Latin Kings, because of our friendly association with quite a few of them, Jose figured he could rock their colors on the reg. I could imagine what their conversation must have been like inside the car.

"Yo D, you saw that?" One of the guys from the back seat would ask.

"Hell yeah," Dusty would answer.

"What are you guys talking about?" Farib would ask.

"That young buck that was walking over there, I think he's LK," Ceasar most likely added.

Farib probably then stepped on the brake immediately and looked out the passenger side mirror. It wouldn't have taken long before he'd

spotted Jose who was near the pay phone now. Not

for nothing, but the kid was a big fat shit.

"Who? That big fat shit right there?" He would say.

"Yeah. We should damage him," Carlos probably egged

on.

"Word," Ceasar was sure to agree.

Jose said he grabbed the phone off the hook and

proceeded to put a quarter into the coin slot. He had

taken out his black colored wallet with a bright

yellow Pac-Man symbol on the front. It was yet

another item with the same color scheme that wasn't

going to help the dilemma he was about to get into.

Inside his wallet, he kept a white piece of paper with

several phone numbers written on it. These were the

numbers to various pay phones around the area from which we sold our drugs. Jose was the only one in the crew who hadn't memorized them yet, therefore having to constantly look at his paper in order to get in contact with me or the others.

The last page he'd received was "911" followed by the number three. This was the number assigned to the park. As he began to dial the number, Ceasar had supposedly walked up behind him.

"Yo my man, hurry up, I need to use the phone," he said.

"Yeah well, I just got here, so…" Jose said he answered as he shrugged his shoulders, brushing off the request.

Suddenly, the bandana Jose had was yanked out of his pocket. He said he quickly spun around with an attitude and snapped back, "Yo, what the fuck is wrong with you?"

With that said, Ceasar had grabbed him by the mouth and pushed his head back into the phone.

"Mira… look at this little man thinking he's tough," Ceasar taunted.

He then grabbed Jose by his coat and pulled him away from the booth letting the phone bang against the side and dangle.

The sound of someone's voice was faintly heard talking on the other line, he had said. Jose alertly scanned his surroundings, it was him against four others. It wouldn't be easy trying to run so he had no other choice but to throw his hands up in the air and get into a fighting stance.

"So, what's up? Come on let's do this," he said he barked at his aggressors. They all seemed to laugh at his heroic effort of seeming unafraid.

Meanwhile, Duckie held a phone in his hand yelling into the receiver, but got no response. All he could hear were various curses and taunts, all of which didn't sound like someone was horsing around. He quickly turned towards the benches.

"Ant, something is going on!" He yelled back at me.

I quickly jumped off the bench and bolted towards the pay phone and snatched it out of Duckie's hand. I pressed the receiver to my ear, "Hello? Hello? Jose!" I screamed out but couldn't hear anything.

•••••••••

Jose had managed to push Carlos up against a wall maneuvering himself just enough to get passed him and Dusty. He ran as fast as he could for half a block with the four teens in hot pursuit but was eventually pushed from behind by Farib, he explained. With that, Jose said he was quickly hurled forward a couple of extra feet, crashing to the pavement. Instinct had Jose putting his hands out in front of him to try and break his fall. Both his palms scraped the concrete, instantly ripping his skin and beginning to bleed. He was half defeated as there would be no chance of him making a fist now and fighting back. The four teens stood over Jose as he cowered in pain. Farib now approached him and without saying a word proceeded to punch him square in the face.

The blow rocked Jose's head back as he threw his hands in front of him attempting to block what was surely to be a barrage of hits, he said. The teens unloaded combinations of punches and kicks that came from all angles. They pounced and pummeled Jose into a swollen and bloody mess. Jose said he just lay on the ground in agony, but definitely wasn't crying.

"Look at this little bitch, crying like a girl," Dusty taunted. This detail I'd heard many years later from someone who happened to witness the attack.

"He's going to be crying for a while," Farib would add.

Farib began to dig in Jose's coat pockets and quickly found the game.

"Oh shit, look what we have here. Yo Carlos, didn't your brother want this one?" Farib asked his homeboy.

"Hell yeah, man. Ghouls and ghosts. Thanks, little bro," Carlos then snatched the bag from Farib's hand, excitedly.

Farib continued searching Jose's coat but found nothing else. He then began searching his pants pockets, pulling out a few twenty dollar bills mixed with the electronic store receipt. He checked his back pockets and found the weed. Farib was astounded that this young boy was in possession of such quantity of marijuana. As he opened the bag and smelled inside, Jose began to fuss and fidget he told me.

"You can't take that you son of a bitch," Jose said he yelled out. Adamant that he fought back tooth and nail until the very end.

"Yeah motherfucker? I already have," Farib supposedly said with a smile.

Apparently after that, Jose said he blanked out. The same witness mentioned earlier also stated Jose had been viciously kicked in the back of the head, knocking him out cold.

••••••••••

At the time of the drama, my heart raced with anticipation. I had experienced so many things in my short life and knew for sure what I was feeling at the moment wasn't good. Meanwhile, Pedro had walked over to the payphone and called one of his friends that lived not too far. He had also ordered for Rosemary and the other girls to head on home while the guys and I quickly headed in the opposite direction. We anxiously awaited by the entrance of the park. The fellas all carried on, each of them speaking about the many different theories for what may have happened to Jose. More importantly, what they were going to do about the situation. I, on the other hand, remained quiet just pacing back and forth. Just like Rolando did.

We must have waited around no more than twenty minutes when a blue van came racing up the block and screeched to a stop in front of us. Wilson, a friend of Pedro's and a member of the Latin King family was behind the wheel. He quickly rolled down the window and told the group to get inside the vehicle. Pedro rode in front, while we all hopped into the back.

The ride was uncomfortable to say the least. The boys desperately tried to hold on for dear life as the van seemed to speed across town whipping turn after turn. The fact that there were no seats in the back only added to the discomfort.

Wilson worked for an uncle of his doing moving jobs and sometimes delivering automotive parts to various mechanics. This explained a big piece of cardboard that covered the floor, blotted with oil stains throughout. I frequently looked down, checking my jeans and making sure I wasn't getting dirty. I remember Taz glancing over at me. Besides not wanting to ruin my jeans, Taz could sense something else was wrong with me.

"You alright? You've been pretty quiet man," he asked.

"I'm cool," I said to him with a blank stare.

The reality was that the events unfolding had me heavily thinking about many things. I'd already heard the multiple stories of retaliatory bragging from my friends' mouths, but what would I do? If something had truly and badly happened to Jose, what kind of revenge would I inflict on the culprits? I thought about all kinds of things and yet there was something still bothering me. Something more profound. Suddenly, the van came to a stop.

Taz scooted towards the back of the van and took a peek out the window.

"I think we're near Jerome," he said. I could hear Pedro's voice talking to someone on the street as him and Wilson got out of the vehicle. While they continued talking, I was clearly able to make out the words "ambulance" and "police". Not a good combination. After a few seconds the side door to the van slid opened and Pedro looked inside.

"What's going on? Taz said.

"I need you guys to get out of here," Pedro ordered.

"What happened? Why are we getting out?" I asked.

"Look, Filipo just told us there's a bunch of police and shit blocking the street. I don't want to roll with you's in the van just in case they stop us. You know what I'm saying?" Pedro explained.

With that said, we slowly hopped out of the van one by one. I shook my head in disbelief, the words *police and shit* constantly being replayed in my mind. This definitely wasn't good news at all.

At this time, Joel walked up the block. He was yet another one of Pedro's Latin King brothers who seemed hyper at all the drama unfolding. I'd seen him before and even sold to him. Joel walked straight up to Pedro and greeted him with the customary and intricate handshake all Latin King members used as salutations.

"Amor del rey," Joel shared "King's love" with Pedro and Wilson. He was greeted with the same by both. Joel now looked over at me with a stressed look on his face.

"Ant. They got your boy, el gordito. They fucked that chubby dude up good, B," he told me.

"Shit," is all I could say to myself as I stared back at him.

"Who did it?" Pedro asked.

"I think it was those cats from MS."

"Yo, I swear man, we gonna fuck them up," Wilson screamed in anger.

Meanwhile, I had finally heard the inevitable. Jose had been jumped and beat up. And while everyone else had their adrenaline kicked up a notch, I slowly walked away and placed my back against a wall. My head was down and I was somewhat depressed. One of my best friends had been beaten up, so badly that the ambulance had to come for him. One of the Foo's was put down. Jose out of all people, possibly the strongest one in the crew. *If he got jumped and beat up, that could definitely mean another thing. Had he gotten robbed?* I thought to myself. Then it finally dawned on me. That something else I kept thinking about. The real reason why I was so upset and bothered.

"Fuck. They took the weed," I remember whispering to myself.

What kind of friend was I? I had just learned that Jose had gotten roughed up pretty badly and yet the fact that an ounce of weed, my motherfucking weed was now missing, was what was absolutely killing me. That's all I could think about. I had never dealt with anything like this. But I knew I had to do something about it. This was my time to show what kind of person I was, no matter my age. I couldn't let it slip by. This was the test I had heard about in the past. If you got hit, you definitely had to hit back harder. Pedro wanted to get back at the MS guys because that's what gangs did. I did too; after all, I chose to sell drugs, so there was no way I was going to allow anybody to fuck with me or my crew, ever.

•••••••••

Jose ended up spending two days in the hospital. Lucky for him the swelling of his face was the worst of his beating. He had no broken bones, nor did he need any stitches, and his hands would eventually heal on their own given some time. All his mother ever knew about the incident was that their sweet and innocent little boy was the victim who got jumped by gang members and nothing more.

For showing toughness and never flinching when asked questions by police officers and his mom, the crew all chipped in and bought Jose his game which was stolen. Everyone except me. It wasn't that I was bitter, and I didn't greet Jose with any ill will, but the fact remained that I had lost money. I was slowly showing signs of the person I would fast become. The whole drug thing was strictly business now.

It was exactly one week later that Pedro would summon me and the rest of the group to meet up with him at his apartment. It pertained to some important

information about Farib and his whereabouts.

Rosemary had formed a strong inkling on what that

whole meeting was about because of her overhearing

a conversation between Pedro and Wilson.

Apparently someone from the Latin Kings network of

members had done some surveillance and struck gold

by finding out where Farib lived. In order to make a

statement, in order to let people, know what the Latin

Kings stood for, Pedro wanted to bring problems

right to where Farib resided and he was going to

bring me along with him.

This was just as much a revenge plot for me and

my friends as it was for the Latin Kings. It was my

friend that was beaten up, it was my weed that was

stolen. Pedro was only laying down the ground work,

paving a nice road for me to follow so that I could seek retribution.

We went over to Pedro's one Saturday night and Rosemary answered the door. She appeared to be infuriated as she stared at me, while I stood in the hallway of her building with the rest of the fellas. We immediately walked right passed her and into the apartment without saying a word, heading straight towards Pedro's room.

The so-called meeting went on for several hours that night. The group was extensively trying to come up with the best way to roll up on Farib when he least expected it. Rosemary said to me sometime later that she couldn't help but place her ear to the locked door, trying her best to pick up tidbits of what we talked about. This particular night she was barred from entering her brother's room because of the nature of the meeting.

It was now a little past one in the morning. Rosemary said she lay on her bed, her eyes half closed. The room was dark except for the lights flashing from the television. She had fallen asleep somewhere between a comedy skit and the second musical performance by Tracy Chapman on "Saturday Night Live". She was suddenly awakened by the sound of Pedro's door slamming. Rosemary then leaped off her bed and turned the volume down on her television. She heard Pedro's voice saying goodbye to me and Duckie. The last two people to leave the apartment. She quickly opened her door to her room and stepped out. As she walked into the kitchen, she glanced over at me and gave me an icy stare.

Duckie and I headed towards the front door when I suddenly stopped.

"Duck, give me a second," I told him. I then turned around and headed for the kitchen.

I stuck my head into the kitchen but Rosemary wasn't there. I quickly looked around, noticing a window that was opened. Rosemary often found solitude in the kitchen by sometimes opening the window and hanging out on the fire escape. I now walked over and stuck my head out. I saw Rosemary sitting on the escape with her feet between the bars dangling over the ledge.

"Are you crazy right now? Its freezing outside. You're going to get sick," I said to her.

"I don't care. Leave me alone Antonio, I'm not in the mood," Rosemary fired back.

"Can I talk to you?" I asked.

"For what? Didn't you do enough talking already with my brother and your dumbass friends?" She said to me.

"They're your friends, too," I answered sarcastically.

"Whatever, Antonio," she huffed.

At this point I knew I was being left with no other choice but to climb out the window in order to speak with Rosemary. I slowly put one foot on a long flat piece of plywood that lay across the radiator that was in front of the window. Building heating was the worst. A housing complex either had no heat at all, or it felt like it consumed an entire apartment in a hundred degrees of pure blazing fire.

The key to climbing out successfully was avoiding contacting the radiator, something Rosemary had perfected a long time ago. With a little exertion, I had managed to slip one leg out the window as the rest of my body followed.

"This is bullshit," I complained.

"No one told you to come outside. I told you to leave me alone, didn't I?" Rosemary said.

"Why are you acting like this?" I asked as I sat next to her.

"Are you serious? You ignored me the whole night. You even walked right past me when you first got here and you're asking me why I'm mad?" She yelled at me.

"I had to talk to your brother, you know that," I continued.

"So, when did that make it right for you to treat me like shit, like if I didn't exist?" Rosemary was furious.

"I'm sorry," I had to apologize.

"Fuck you, Antonio. I don't care if you're sorry or not anymore. You promised me. You said this had nothing to do with you and now look? What are you trying to prove?" Rosemary said with a concerned tone in her voice.

"I don't know, Rosemary. I just have to do something. Look, if I don't do anything then people are going to think I'm a punk," I said to her.

"That's what you're concerned about, your freaking rep? You could do so much better Antonio," she tried to persuade me.

"Like what? I don't care about school. You don't understand. I'm not as smart as you and Abraham, so forget about the books and stuff. I probably won't even graduate. All I know is that I like making money," I added.

"So, that's it for you? You're going to be a drug dealer for the rest of your life?" She questioned.

"I don't know what I'm going to do when I get old. But, I know what I want to do right now," I said as I began to slowly get up and head for the window.

I could feel Rosemary's eyes on me. When I turned, and looked at her, I saw the tears starting to swell. She fought them the best she could, but it was useless. Rosemary was an emotional kind of girl. I just looked at her and turned and started to put one leg back in the window.

"I care about you, Antonio. I care a lot about you. I even think I love you," Rosemary said to me.

I stopped in my tracks and turned back towards her. I could clearly see the pain in her eyes. She was actually pouring her heart out to me. I then responded with a very fucked up answer, I guess, "I'm sorry Rosemary. It's just that… I don't even think I know what love means." I proceeded to climb through the window and back into the kitchen. As I walked away, I could hear Rosemary crying uncontrollably.

••••••••••

Rosemary first told me how she felt that night on the fire escape. She said she loved me. Frankly, I don't even know how she cared for me so much. I never made anything easy for her and yet she stuck by my side through piles of shit. I never bitched to anybody.

Eddie Cisneros

Not once in my life did I ever play the sympathy card

for the things I went through growing up as a child.

But, the fact was that I really didn't know how to

love. I never got it from my mother, nor from

Rolando. Thinking about it, I kind of lacked a lot of

different emotions. One of them being fear. After a

while, I sort of grew numb to a hand being raised in

the air. I didn't even flinch. Caring about someone or

feeling remorse was another one. That's what I found

out the night we rolled up on Farib.

Wilson drove that night and had the balls to park

right in front of where Farib lived. It was me, Pedro,

Wilson, Duckie, and Carl. We waited for a couple of

hours until Carl spotted Farib walking up the block

with his girlfriend. She was this square backed bitch

who appeared to be fresh off a boat or plane with no

papers. She was pregnant at that. As the two were about to go up some stairs, we all jumped out of the car and surrounded them.

Carl quickly ran behind the girl and wrapped his arm around her neck. Pedro and Wilson stood in front of Farib cursing and threatening him. I stood in back with Duckie. Suddenly, Pedro looked at me and gave an approving nod. I had been holding a rusty lead pipe in my hand the entire time, which I then raised in the air. Whether I was blinded by anger or the adrenaline rushing through my body, I never thought twice about any consequences. I simply reacted on impulse and swung the pipe. As it crashed against the back of Farib's skull, all I heard was a great big "POP". What made matters worse was that I did it again and again.

Three blows dropped Farib to the ground. A puddle of blood began to form around his head as his girlfriend screamed hysterically. The rest of the guys then moved in and started kicking him. They inflicted on Farib the same dose he had brought upon Jose, but with more intensity, more rage. I looked down at the ground with a blank stare until Wilson grabbed me and shoved me into the car. As we sped off, I remember looking back at Farib, he didn't appear to be moving as his girlfriend was on her knees crying and screaming for help.

We all take actions in life whether they're good or bad. And when you do unto others, sometimes some people don't forget. I was going to have a lot more of that to look forward to for the rest of my life.

....

Mildred lay on her bed half asleep, her mouth semi-opened. Her illness wasn't improving and practically had her bedridden now. As she breathed in and out several times, she suddenly woke up gasping for air and began to cough. She sat up in her bed desperately trying to clear her throat, until she was able to rustle up some phlegm from her chest and into her mouth. She looked around the bed and found a tissue which she used to spit into. She remained seated for a while until she finally exerted enough strength to get off the bed and stand up.

Mildred shuffled her feet towards a bureau and stood in front of a mirror looking at her reflection. The image that stared back at her was an ugly one. Mildred looked in the mirror up and down and turned her face side to side, examining her aging and pockmarked skin and a sore near her mouth which seemed fresh.

Mildred now opened her mouth wide, staring at the but six teeth she had left. This sight was too much for her to bear as she broke down and began to sob. It was the AIDS that was bringing on the joint pains, the pneumonia, and the sores. It was her extensive heroin use in life that contributed to her bad skin and gum disease that made her teeth fall out at the mere bite into an apple. Mildred couldn't help but cry. She felt like she was slowly transforming into a horrid looking monster as the sickness took over her body.

Suddenly, the front door to the apartment slammed. Mildred quickly looked at the door and got a glimpse of Antonio walking past the room. He headed directly for the bathroom as he turned the light on and locked the door.

"Antonio, what are you doing? Why are you coming home so late?" He heard his mother saying from her room.

Antonio ignored her question and remained quiet. He had other problems right now instead of answering why he was so tardy. He looked down at both of his hands, still shocked to see dried up blood on them.

Antonio removed his hooded sweater and tossed it on the floor near the tub. He now leaned in and stood over the sink. Antonio quickly turned on the faucets and immediately ran his hands under the water. He reached for a bar of soap and began to furiously scrub his hands attempting to wash off the blood.

Meanwhile, Mildred continued standing in front of the mirror. She reached down in front of her and dabbed some lotion onto her hands. She then slathered it all over on both sides really working the lotion into the creases of her palms and then her knuckles. Once her hands were smooth, she reached down and pumped the lotion bottle once more, this next glob was for her face which she proceeded to massage.

She started with her cheeks, moving underneath her eyes and then to her forehead. For the first time in a long time Mildred had found some energy and used it to try and somewhat pamper herself. She was slowly starting to feel better, even managing to crack a half smile.

Mildred now decided to open the top drawer on her bureau and pulled out a brown colored jewelry box. She quickly opened it and rustled whatever trinkets she had inside until the she dug way down to the bottom.

She managed to grab a Polaroid picture that was hidden beneath her jewelry and took it out of the box. It was a photo of Troy. He posed with his hands crossed out in front of his chest, standing in front of Coney Island's famed Cyclone rollercoaster.

Mildred stared at the photo for a while until she raised it to her mouth and kissed it. She now closed her eyes thinking about her one true love, her only true love.

As she opened her eyes, the image in the mirror staring back was suddenly different. Mildred finally saw herself as this beautiful young woman. There were no pockmarks on her cheeks, no wrinkles on her forehead and near the corners of her eyes. Her skin was absolutely flawless.

Her smile had widened as she closed her eyes once again. Mildred was able to visualize she and Troy holding hands. Troy was gorgeous. He was this finely featured gentleman with a charismatic smile and a pumped up physique. The two of them walked until Troy suddenly stopped and faced her. He then leaned in caressing her face and finally kissing her softly on the lips.

As Troy pulled away he was suddenly wearing a dashing black tuxedo. Both of them were in a church standing at the altar in front of a priest. Mildred glanced over at the pews seeing her mother and father beaming back at her. They appeared to be extremely happy. Her and Troy now turned and began to walk down a set of stairs and down the aisle. This dream of hers felt so real that she remained with her eyes closed. Mildred feared that if she opened them, all would be lost.

The two had walked the full length of the church as she reached out and opened the door to leave. On the other side, Mildred now fantasized that she was pregnant. Her and Troy were walking barefoot in a park as he playfully rubbed on her stomach. They came to a spot underneath a tree and laid down together. Troy just stared at her as he ran his fingers through her golden hair.

"You know I love you right?" He whispered to her.

"I love you too, baby," Mildred replied.

Mildred stood in front of the mirror, her eyes remaining closed as she nodded her head in agreement to the question her vision of Troy had just asked.

Suddenly, Mildred was lying in a hospital bed with her legs wide open and propped upwards. Troy stood by her side holding her hands as a doctor asked for her to push. Her intense pain of giving birth finally turned into a sob of emotional joy as the doctor held Mildred's new baby in his hands.

A nurse quickly grabbed the baby in her mind, wrapping it in a blanket and placing the child in a resuscitation trolley while she cleaned and removed mucus. Mildred's face was sweaty and exhausted.

Imaginary Troy clutched her hands as he kissed her on the cheek. His eyes filled with tears at the sight of his newborn. The nurse finally walked back over towards the bed and let Mildred hold her baby for the first time. It was a joyous occasion. The beaming couple had just received their first child into the world. A brand new and beautiful little baby girl.

Mildred's head occasionally swayed back as she continued to stand. It had been a while that she was able to escape and transcend her mind into her perfect dream world. Whenever she did, it usually was the same dream she would have. The perfect husband in Troy. The perfect relationship in marriage and parenthood, her little baby daughter.

She dreamt of holding her as an infant and even seeing the girl grown up as she stood in back of her brushing her hair. This was the real life Mildred had always wanted. Dreaming about it was the only way to get it.

Antonio flushed his face with water as he looked up and stared at his reflection in the mirror. The beads of water rolled off his cheeks and into the sink as he stood there watching himself without blinking. He was starting to feel better.

Antonio closed the faucets and reached for a towel to dry off. The events that night were beginning to fade away more and more. His face was cleaned, so were his hands. Any noticeable evidence of his violent actions had long spiraled down the drain and just like that, everything felt good again.

Antonio exited the bathroom and headed for his room. As he was about to enter, something inside him felt the need to turn towards his mother's room.

"Goodnight mom," he said as he finally entered his room and shut the door.

Mildred suddenly opened her eyes, startled upon hearing Antonio's bedroom door close. She looked around her room squinty-eyed, no one was there. Her knees buckled a bit as she placed her hands on the

bureau for balance. She took one last look at the photo

of Troy that she had taken out. Mildred then

managed to look at her right arm and the needle that

stuck out of it.

Her eyelids grew heavy once again. Mildred closed

them; it was now back to her dream world. Mildred

drifted back to that perfect life she had always

desperately wanted.

Chapter 9

"His-Story Lesson"

Trevor Higgins was one pumped up son of a bitch. That's how he was described by detective Carlos Acevedo two years earlier during a routine license plate check.

Trevor was pulled over one night for running a red light on Pennsylvania Avenue in Brooklyn. The detective hit pay dirt, when the information he got back was that Higgins had been driving with no car insurance. It seemed like every cop in Brooklyn was out to find anything they could in order to mess with Higgins and his NLT crew.

Nobody could blame the cops. Higgins liked to drive around town in an all-black BMW with blue neon lights emitting from underneath the vehicle.

Drawing attention to himself wasn't that difficult.

Higgins was of Jamaican decent being born in Kingston, although he didn't speak with any kind of accent. That part of his heritage would only be on display if she were mad, usually berating someone in the crew, someone he had beef with, or the police which he referred to as the "Putrid One-Time".

He likened the entire law enforcement and judicial systems to "Babylon", stating that no matter what, they would always be forever corrupt. He had a knack for putting his words together so poignantly that one could easily fall into believing he was a victim in the way police dealt with him. That's how good he was.

At 6'8, Trevor had the height to intimidate anyone. He weighed roughly 240lbs of pure solidness. Many people speculated that Trevor began a regimen of steroidal use back in high school where he played varsity football, although he never outright admitted anything.

The people around him never even brought the subject up out of fear. A girlfriend he once had by the name of Dolores let some rumor slip out about his testes being smaller than normal and shriveled in appearance. Dolores suddenly disappeared one day never to be heard of again.

It had now gone on six months since the big police bust that netted nothing against NLT or the Rosa family. But the fact remained that both parties suffered huge profit losses, all masterminded by Marlon.

This had been confirmed by several people in and around Brooklyn. Marlon Nathaniel White was known by many to be a snake in the grass, finding all types of convoluted schemes to make some cash. At one point, NLT had opened their arms to him, allowing Marlon to be a part of the group.

He initially started out as a lookout graduating to actually selling some product. Marlon was getting keen on the idea of being known as a drug dealer, more so because he rolled with the New Lots circle who meant serious business. They were about pumping drugs and making money by any means necessary. The crew was about controlling a large area and not allowing anyone else to move in.

NLT were a vicious bunch when they had to be. Trevor had found a way to control two-thirds of the building he resided in by paying off the superintendents and porters.

NLT had six different apartments within several floors of each other, not including regular units where close friends or family lived. This form of chaos always threw police off if they were involved with chasing or tracking down a suspect. One could easily escape by knocking on someone's door and laying low for a while.

For a good long time, Marlon was doing everything right. He was regarded by Trevor and many in the group as a stand-up guy, very dependable. That was up to the day that Lamont Jordan was released from prison. Marlon slowly saw a shift in power angling in favor of Lamont. The fact that he was Trevor's cousin also wasn't helping.

Suddenly, Marlon wasn't called upon to handle certain deals with other dealers or suppliers. He had never much displayed an angry or violent side, always taking on more of a business approach. But there were times when pressure was needed and that attitude was second nature to Lamont. He was able to handle those situations with ease.

With Lamont's rapid rise to stardom, Marlon knew that he was being pushed aside, therefore he needed something big in order to impress Trevor. One night, through exhaustive means of contacting people, Marlon was able to set up a meeting between NLT and some Colombian guys who he had befriended during his run as a deal maker.

The legalities of the meeting were going to be simple enough. Several bricks of uncut cocaine for a very decent and low price. It was a deal that would eventually go down, sans Marlon who was advised to leave any intimidating talking or tactics to Lamont. Marlon knew right there and then he wasn't someone Trevor relied on anymore. He felt bitter and angry, betrayed. He had gone above and beyond to set up a nice deal for Trevor and was even cut short of some money.

Trevor was sprawled out on a leather couch with one hand on the remote control, the other down his pants occasionally scratching. He sat there flicking through several channels until he found something to hold his interest for a few minutes.

At this time, Lamont walked into the living room and approached Trevor.

"Tre, what's good?" He said.

Trevor continued watching television not saying a word. Lamont eased in some more and started to sit down on a leather loveseat. Trevor then slowly looked over at him, somewhat irked.

"Did I ever ask you to take a fucking seat?" Trevor asked.

"Nah, man," Jordan replied.

"So why the fuck are you sitting then?" Trevor asked, agitated now.

"Tre, I figured…"

"Figured what man? You figured that you could come up in my crib and make yourself comfortable? You want something to eat, something to drink? You want to pipe down my shorty also? It seems lately that all you motherfuckers are real laid back and what not. The fact you coming in here and taking a load off on my motherfucking loveseat is only telling me that you have some good news, because if not we have a shitload of problems, my nigga, related or not," Trevor spoke with anger.

Lamont squirmed a bit but remained seated. He'd already taken the initiative to sit, might as well stay there and at least try and show some toughness.

"Well?" Trevor asked.

"Cats is still working on it."

"So, nothing is what you really saying to me, right?"

"Yeah. But T, check it. I don't know if it's legit or not, but he may have been spotted out in the Bronx, hanging out with some other cat."

"Who told you this?"

"That Spanish nigga, Julio, remember him? He used to live off of Atlantic."

"And that's the only information you have right now? Speculation? Niggas thinking they saw Marlon?"

"T, I'm working on it."

"Yo check this out, Lamont. You better work hard, real motherfucking hard. I want that piece of shit "Batty Bwoy" in front of me. If he's rolling with somebody who thinks they coming up in the world, then bring them too. I want Marlon to see my gun pressed up against his forehead. His peeps can see his fucking brains splatter out through the back of his head. You feeling me? I don't want people telling me they think. I want facts. And if you can't handle that, I guess you may as well disappear just like Marlon. With that said. Get the fuck off my couch, and get the fuck out of my crib," Trevor replied, ending the conversation right there and then.

●●●●●●●●●●

Months after the Farib incident I was still constantly looking over my shoulder. I remember being a nervous mess. Every phone call, every knock on my apartment door made my heart pound. That whole feeling was totally different than the one I felt when selling. This was about having problems. Real straight up beef. We had retaliated on some guy, so who was to say that a group of his people weren't going to roll up on me and get even? These weren't the things a boy of my age was supposed to be thinking about and yet it took over my life day and night.

I desperately tried not to let anyone ever see me pressing the issue or acting like I was scared. Truth was, I was scared to death. On some evenings once I was the only one left and had to walk home by myself, I admit I ran all the way to my building like a shot out of a fucking canon. If Rosemary wanted to hang out, I made excuses for us to stay home and chill. If someone told me to visit, I told them to come to my crib instead. It was out of fear that I acted this way in the beginning. But, only years later did I finally come to realize — that's the way of life for all drug dealers.

We do our dirt and yet hide in the shadows. We become the wizard from OZ, standing behind a curtain, manipulating every little step and all movements of our soldiers. And we remain behind the scenes while everything around us falls into place.

At least this is the mentality of the smart drug dealers, the ones that actually stick around for a while. My soldiers back then were the likes of Duckie, Carl, Jose, and Taz. They listened to what I spoke about with real interest, they believed in me and did what I asked.

While I was fretting about bashing some kids head in, Duckie and Taz took a bulk of the weed and kept it with them. Duckie had no problem hiding anything from his parents. His mother was a functioning alcoholic and his pops worked late, came home fucked his wife whenever he felt like it and would disappear on weekends.

Taz? Well let's just say having a militant and Muslim
father didn't help our cause. Taz's father ended up finding a good amount of stuff in Taz's room. He

requested to speak with me. The lesson I was taught

was something I would never forget.

He helped me to understand who I really was.

··········

I slowly walked in through the front door and was

immediately greeted with three elegantly hand

carved masks made out of wood hanging on the

hallway wall. They were of a tiger, a giraffe, and a

zebra. Once in the living room, it was like visiting a

full blown art gallery of Afrocentric culture. I was

quickly enthralled at the museum-like pieces the

living room was fitted with. There were paintings and

statues of African Maasai women and children. A

statue of a Maasai warrior holding a spear in his hand

ready to strike.

On the opposite side of the room the displays harked back into Egyptian times with paintings of Queen Isis and Nefertiti, little statues of sphinxes and Ushabti figurines, and a heavy looking bust of King Tutankhamen that sat on a wooden table. I couldn't help but notice that the statues eyes seemed to follow me wherever I walked.

On yet another wall there hung a flag representing the nation of Islam. It was a solid red color with the shapes of a crescent moon and star in white. I walked over to the wall and just looked at the flag. I observed the four letters that were emblazoned on the four corners of it. In the top left hand corner was the letter "J", the top right hand corner was the letter "F". On the bottom left hand corner was the letter "E", with the letter "I" on the other side.

No sooner than I had reached out and ran my finger over the letters to feel every stitch, did I hear Taz's father say to me, "The letters stand for freedom, justice, equality, and Islam."

"Ah, I'm sorry sir. I didn't mean to disrespect you by touching the flag," I said nervously backing away from the wall.

"It's cool, young blood. Asalaam alaikum," Saif greeted me.

"Lakum salam," I quickly answered back.

"Why don't you come into the kitchen?" Saif instructed.

The two of us sat in the kitchen; I remember having my hands neatly folded out in front of me as if I were back in elementary school. As much of badasses as we thought we were, many of Taz's friends, including myself, always showed respect to his father. Saif was of medium build and in his mid-forties. It was never a question of his size but more for the way that he carried himself that garnered this respect shown to him. He was always serious, but fair. Saif wore black rimmed glasses and sported a nappy salt and pepper goatee as he put a licorice root chew stick into his mouth. He then looked over at me.

"You want one?" He asked.

"No, sir," I replied.

"They're cinnamon flavored. They're actually good for your teeth. Did you know that?" He asked again.

"Yes sir," I agreed.

"Call me Saif, please," he was being polite.

"Taz, I mean Tazeem told me about the sticks one day," I explained.

Up to that point, I'd maintained looking down at the table. It was probably evident that I was slightly nervous, although I tried to fight it the best I could.

"You know why I asked to speak with you right?" Saif asked.

"Yes, I do," I replied. I knew very well why he wanted to speak with me.

"I'll deal with Tazeem later on, but I wanted to square things up with you first. That's a lot of weed little man. If you're selling it for someone else, I didn't want you to get into some nonsense over it. Then my son comes out and tells me it's yours. And I'm saying to myself, *where in the world does a child your age get so much smoke from?*" Saif said.

At that moment I had suddenly gone silent. I just sat there biting my bottom lip.

"You're not gonna answer that, huh? It's cool. I give it to you man, you're definitely disciplined. For that I have to give you respect," Saif said.

"Thank you," I said without sounding sarcastic or anything.

"You do know that your discipline you have could eventually bring you to a place not so good, right? You could end up becoming a statistic, and nothing more," Saif explained.

"I know," I replied.

"That's what you want, little man? Is that what you really want? It's what they want. You see me being a black man; I could raise my voice and scream about the injustice I feel and how people treat me bad and all that rhetoric, but I won't and I don't. Again, that's what they want me to do. It's the white folks that run this country, that's who I'm talking about.

They want us to make noise, so that they can say,

'You see, these little apes and niggers don't know

how to behave, that's why they need to be kept in

line.' And you being Hispanic, you're no better. You

know why? It's the simple fact that you're a minority.

All of us. And as long as we're the minority in this

country, well man, we ain't worth shit! They want

you to sell your weed to other 'Spics. They want us all

to keep buying beer and liquor, cigarettes, and drugs

and guns, and then keep us all together living in the

same community. That's a grim scope of

demographics right there for you. They don't want

you to progress, none of us," Saif spoke with a stern

voice.

The more he spoke, the less I fidgeted and the

more I looked him in the eyes.

"People might go around and say that I'm crazy. My attitude is let them believe that. But, you see I read books and constantly try and feed my brain knowledge. It's that same knowledge that I try and pass on to Tazeem. I know that you little thunder cats think that you're hot news and the words I try and preach are gonna go in through one ear and out the other, but it's okay. That's a part of being a child and growing up and learning things on your own. But, you kids need to wise up and build your minds, elevate it to something bigger and better. If you keep up the nonsense you're doing, all you continue to do is prove to them that we're lower," Saif explained.

At this time, I remember reaching into my pocket and taking out a box of "Chiclets" chewing gum. I opened the yellow box and poured two tablets into my hand and into my mouth.

"I see a lot of you's walking around and it's sad sometimes because you children are being fed lies. You see life from just one side of things. Take for instance those sneakers you guys like wearing. How much do they go for?" He asked me.

"I don't know, maybe a hundred and thirty, hundred and fifty. It depends," I told him.

"Did you know those sneakers right there probably cost twenty, maybe thirty dollars to make. Their probably made in some poor-ass country by workers who get paid cents even. And you kids want to go out and spend top dollar for them, kill each other over them just because they're branded with some logo. What about that gum right there, you know about that?" He said to me.

"Gum? No. I just buy it because I like them," I answered.

"I heard a funny story about that right there one time, but it made sense the more I kept thinking about it. The story supposedly comes directly from Hispanic blood line in the Mayans. They used to chew this kind of sap from a sapodilla tree. They called it chicle. Along comes some American inventor by the name of John Adams, a white man of course, and he starts to fidget around with chicle thinking it could be used as an alternative to rubber. Eventually he finds out its better used to chew on. You see, you chew it, yes, because like you said, you like the taste. But, there's real history behind a lot of shit you kids don't know about it," Saif said.

I quickly grabbed the box of gum and examined it from all angles. "That's crazy," I replied.

"Damn right it's crazy and you better believe it. We are all conditioned to listen to one thing, one point of view and that's it. But, this is their history.

It's like Christopher Columbus. You know who that is

right?" Saif asked.

"He discovered America," I said with enthusiasm

while propped up in my seat.

"One side of the story, if you want to believe that.

Other people believe Columbus was a racist

oppressor. He eventually fought and killed people

that were already here, minorities if you will, and

stole their possessions, whether it be land or gold,

whatever," Saif countered.

After that, I quickly slouched back in my seat. I

looked up at him.

"May I ask you something? I've always noticed

that Tazeem practically does everything with his right

hand. He eats, he shakes hands, he'll give me

something or take it from me, you know regular

things. But as long as I've known him, he does other stuff with his left hand. Like, he'll pick his nose or even touch, well, you know, weed with his left. Why?" I asked.

"Wow, I'm impressed. That's very observant. Disciplined and observant, I kind of underestimated you, little bro. Anyway, Muslims believe the right hand is supposed to be used for good deeds, or just being polite. The left is for cleansing purposes. We believe in the Al Qiyamah, the Day of Judgement, praise be to Allah. As Allah is quoted as saying in the Qur'an, Surah Al Hud, verse 103: 'In that is a sign for those who fear the penalty of the hereafter. That is a day for which mankind will be gathered together. That will be a day of testimony. Nor shall we delay it but for a term appointed.'

We believe in the records of deeds that will be given to people in either their right hand or their left, like in the verse that states: 'As for him who is given his book in his right hand, he shall surely receive an easy reckoning and he will return to his family rejoicing. But as for him who is given his book behind his back, he shall call for destruction on himself and will burn in a blazing fire.' The hand behind one's back is the left. You understand?" Saif explained to me.

"Damn, that's deep shit. I mean deep stuff right there," I answered him.

"All good. You're right though. It is deep shit. First off, Tazeem has it all backwards. Just because the left and right hand have their different meanings, doesn't mean he should be touching or selling or doing anything bad at all. I'll be sure to let him know about himself when I get the chance," Saif said with attitude.

"Tazeem says that Jesus was black. Is that true?" I questioned while Saif just sat there and smiled.

"Man, that's a whole other topic right there, but if you want me try and break it down? You Catholic, right?" Saif asked me.

"I don't know. I think so?" I said hesitantly.

"Yeah, you're Catholic. All you Hispanics are. I believe in Jesus, Isa. But when you break down the whole theory of who he was and where he came from, it's something that makes you think. You know who Noah is?" Saif now asked.

"Hell yeah! It was that dude with the boat, right?" I said exuberantly.

"The ark, son. Well, people believe that all of mankind are descendants from Noah's three sons who were Shem, Ham, and Japheth. Now each of

these sons settled in different places. Japheth basically

settled in Turkey, he then moved around to various

places, ending up in Europe and ultimately in Russia.

So, through Japheth, it is believed the descendants

were Caucasians, white. Ham's descendants were the

people who settled in Africa. You already know what

skin color we talking about? And then there was

Shem, who people believe Jesus was a descendant of,

through his line all the way to Abraham. That line is

extensive. I mean, I can throw names at you like,

Arphaxad, Cainan, Eber, Salah, Reu. Follow me here

now. Shem settled in the areas that are known as

Jordan and Israel, Saudia Arabia and Lebanon. We're

talking about areas of the world that are hot, blazing

sun like a good portion of the day. I mentioned

Abraham; Abraham came from a Sumerian city called

Ur of Chaldees, a black civilization. Did you know that there are descriptions of Jesus in the bible that refer to his hair like wool, his feet of fine brass, which could hint at him being dark skinned?

There are no known pictures of him, and any ones that were drawn came in a time where they were sanctioned by the Roman Catholic Church, a white Anglo-Saxon people. So, of course they're gonna depict him as being a white man. Bottom line is that when you talk about that part of history, that place in time, these people in the bible are described as people with at least olive skin. Hell, Jesus may have been your color for all we know. Hay-Soos, that's what you call him right?" Saif said.

I admit to being confused at all the names being thrown by him, yet, I focused and listened to Saif speak with passion about the subject at hand. This had become a lecture and lesson in history, of religion, that I had never listened to or learned in any school. The rest of that afternoon was spent on talking about various theories Saif had about all kinds of things in life.

What started out as me giving Taz weed to hold, turned out to be some kind of lecture in me having to use my smarts for better things and how I should really stay in school, but find ways to read all the time and just stay ahead of the game on an intellectual level.

I came away from the talking with more of a fucked up perspective at least when it came to religion. Apart from not knowing whether or not I believed in God and Christ, I had to inject into my thought process that Jesus may have been a black man. Maybe even a Puerto Rican or Dominican, or some kind of Hispanic. The one thing I did realize? I got a better perspective on who I was. I'm still that person to this date.

Saif told me how in the white people's eyes he would always be black and inferior, he was straight up a stone cold nigger who would always be a threat to society whether he had a gun in his hand or a book. He said that I would always be a 'Spic, His-panic. The white man would eventually fear me because there was going to come a time when I wasn't considered a minority anymore. We were going to be the majority. I kind of liked that idea. I chose to live my life having people fear me instead of them taking advantage of me and walking all over me.

As far as my weed goes. He ended up giving it

back. He swore up and down it would be the last time

it was going to be in his house. With that lesson? I

didn't really learn a damn fucking thing!

Chapter 10

"Prying Eyes"

Rolando walked out of a grocery store with several bags in hand. He made his way to the back of a shiny, newly waxed Lincoln Continental. Sitting inside the vehicle was Chester who reached over and popped open the trunk for Rolando.

While many people that lived in impoverished neighborhoods depended on food stamps for their grocery shopping, Rolando could often walk into any supermarket once a month and engage in a hundred and fifty or more dollars' worth of food and other needed supplies for the household. He kept himself always looking dapper, preferring to dress in slacks and shoes on a constant basis, even for groceries.

He sported jewelry of all sorts, dangling from his neck and wrists. He always smelled good, an aromatic assortment of different cologne's that would elicit a smile or two from some women.

Meanwhile, Chester tapped his hands on the steering wheel to the sounds of salsa music playing on the radio. He was in good spirits as he mouthed the words to the song, really getting into it.

Life was treating the likes of Rolando, Chester, and Marlon well with business showing no signs of slowing down. Chester was another one who was beginning to incorporate Rolando's code of dress, also wearing expensive shirts and shoes.

Rolando often joked around with Chester by asking him if he were going to some business meeting or appointment. His sudden outlook on clothing and appearance had to do with Rolando convincing him to maintain a certain look, even getting Chester to drop his feral bushy beard and always have it neat and trimmed up. The attitude behind it was, *"So what about your scar. It gives a person something to look at. It gives them something to be afraid of."* Ever since then, Chester had been visiting a local barber on a regular basis.

Rolando eased into the seat and closed the door. He then looked over at Chester.

"I need you to pass by Kiko's. If you like, you can leave me there," he said.

"What's up with that fool?" Chester asked.

"He's good. He just found some new connect, he wants me to meet her tonight."

"Her? Knowing Kiko it sounds like he's gonna end up trying to fuck her."

"Well, he can try, but as far as what I've heard from some people, she's real tough. I don't think she gets fucked. I think she likes doing the fucking."

"That kind of sounds like the fat piece of shit girlfriend he used to have."

"Used to? She still is."

The two shared a laugh as Chester began to pull out from the parking spot. About three cars' length down, a black four door Acura with tinted windows also pulled out of a spot and kept some distance behind Chester's car so as not to be noticed.

With every left and right turn Chester made, with every red light he stopped at, the Acura did the same remaining not too far behind. Chester would finally pull up to a brownstone building. Meanwhile, the Acura passed them and continued towards the end of the block quickly pulling up to a fire hydrant and stopping. Rolando now exited the vehicle as he looked to both sides. He then leaned in towards the passenger side window.

"Hey, see if you can pass by the apartment and drop off the groceries. And, check on Millie," he asked Chester.

"Esta bien, I'll do it bro," Chester answered.

"And Chester. Watch your back, you hear me?"

"What's up?"

"Nothing. I just feel jumpy sometimes, you know?"

"Don't worry too much. Everything is cool, papi."

Chester rolled up the window and pulled off, driving to the end of the block. All the while, Rolando kept his eyes on the him as he watched the Lincoln finally turn left and disappear. Rolando then turned to walk towards the building. The Acura suddenly revved its motor, pulling up to the corner and making

a quick left turn.

• • • • • • • • • •

Detectives Redding and Trammel "Casper" sat

quietly in their car. The ghost moniker given to

Tramell by Jordan was already circulating throughout

the precinct and pretty much the streets of Brooklyn.

It had caught on like a wild fire.

It was nine o'clock on the dot, indicated by

Redding's watch as he lay his arm back down on his

lap. He looked over to his side, Tramell's seat was

laid back as he had his eyes closed. The two cops had

been parked outside a dark one way street for an hour

and a half occasionally making eye contact with a

brick house across the street. It was the home of

Shameeka Wilson, one of Lamont's various girlfriends who he was paying a visit to this particular night.

"This is nonsense. We have a ton of other fucks' names as a part of this group, some of them who are probably at the park right now pumping their shit, and we're here playing surveillance for Jordan as he gets his dick sucked?" Redding fumed.

"Nothing yet?" Tramell asked as he opened his eyes and took a peek at the house.

"Nothing yet? Are you fucking serious? There's not a damn light on in that house right now. We're just sitting here like two shmucks."

"Yep well, relax, it's all a part of the game," Tramell said as he sat up, raising the back of the car seat.

"Did I tell you what Lamont is trying to pull off?" Redding asked.

"No. What?"

"Get this, he found some Jew cocksucking lawyer whose plight in life is to help out these bunch of lowlifes. They're filing some suit against the department for failure to acknowledge accordingly that fuck face is an asthmatic. Lamont said the night he spent in Central that he was having chest pains and that no one did anything for him."

"Get the fuck out of here," Tramell said as he smiled.

"I'm serious. The capper is that, the black shit actually does have in his records a history for asthma. If IA gets involved because of any pressure from this lawyer, they're going to have a field day with this one."

"That's nonsense. I read his list of possessions on him that night up and down. There is nothing listed for any asthma pump. There can't possibly be a case there."

"You never know. Saul Weisenberg, that's the lawyer's name. These Jews can squeeze a penny out of a fucking rock, I'm telling you."

Tramell just looked at Redding shaking his head.

"Has anyone ever told you that you exhibit an awfully tremendous amount of hostility? What is it, your lady not hooking you up?" Tramell joked.

"Check this out. Fuck you, and her. How about that?" Redding answered back.

"You see what I mean," Tramell said as he laughed.

At this moment, a black two door Lexus had turned the corner and slowly drove up the block. Gabriel Rosa was behind the wheel as his brother

Frankie looked on either side trying his best to make out the house numbers.

They had neared the middle of the block as Frankie looked to his left, then to his right. He suddenly looked straight ahead, somewhat scared.

"Conio! Sigue, sigue, sigue!" He whispered to his brother, cursing for him go.

"What is it?" Gabriel asked

"Just go, dale!"

Gabriel obliged and stepped on it for sure without asking any more questions. They reached the corner, stopping at the sign and then turned left. Gabriel had driven half way up the avenue and then slowed down.

"What the fuck was that all about?" Gabriel asked.

"Those maldito blanco cops, man. Those damn white pigs were parked outside the house."

"Cuales?"

"That guy Casper and his partner. Mamajuevos, malditos gringos de mierda," Frankie's slurs continued as he called the cops dicksucking white pieces of shit, "I told you man. Those negros are hot. Pa should have never messed with them." Frankie said in a huff.

"Fuck it then. Let's bounce from here before we get into more beef with these cops."

With that said, Gabriel pressed on the gas and drove off.

··········

It was just passed midnight as the black four door Acura quickly pulled into an open spot on the block. The engine revved one last time as the car was finally shut off.

Stepping out of the vehicle was a scrawny looking white gentleman in his mid-forties by the name of Jamison. Nothing more, nothing less, just plain Jamison. Despite the ambiguous single name, his wiry, geeky looking glasses' frames, and his overall appearance, Jamison was known in the underground world of criminal activities and misdeeds as one person you did not want following you around.

In this instance, he had been tailing Rolando, and more so Chester, for a week and two days, intricately detailing Chester's every move in a marble colored notebook which he always carried with him.

Jamison slowly inserted the keys into his front door and walked into his apartment. It was a small apartment, in a very fucked housing complex, in an even more fucked part of the barrio near 116th Street,

Manhattan. But, Jamison didn't care that he lived in a ghetto, nor did he have to.

The entire apartment was dark except for a dim hall light that lead to his bedroom. Jamison liked the dark. He would often sit in a chair in the middle of his living room for hours just facing the front door.

He would stare at the hallway light coming from underneath his door, without moving a single muscle. He would then close his eyes and take in every sound coming from his apartment.

The constant drip, drip from his kitchen sink. The pitter patter of mice scurrying throughout the apartment.

Jamison also knew the sounds coming from his floor. The ding from the elevator doors opening, doors slamming, whether it was his neighbors or someone using the stairwell.

Once inside, Jamison closed his door and slowly walked over to his wall phone; he picked up the receiver. He then dialed a number. As he waited for someone to answer on the other line, he'd already popped a cigarette into his mouth and lit it. He walked over to a window and looked outside.

From the second floor apartment he could see down near the playground and the basketball courts. A bunch of guys were just hanging out near some benches as they listened to music coming from a boom box plopped on it. It was the same group every night. Talking and laughing, occasional hand to hand deals with crackheads and potheads. They were obnoxious and many times raucous, even harassing some people as they attempted to enter or exit the building through the side entrance.

"Hello?" A voice was heard on the other end.

"Con Gabriella, por favor.'

Jamison answered, asking to speak with Gabriella,

using his best attempt to speak in Spanish.

Chapter 11

"Gabriella Braga"

Gabriella Braga was a strikingly gorgeous looking woman that came close to having Amazonian type features. She stood at six, two and easily towered over many of her associates. She was quite curvaceous, had long black hair that reached down passed her waist, and had a smooth caramel complexion that seemed almost flawless except for a minute scar near her left cheek. At any particular meeting, it was easy to catch one or two people, men or women, simply enthralled by her beauty.

And then there was her eyes.

Gabriella had what was called partial heterochromia resulting from a car accident she was in when she was seven years old, she had once told me. Her right eye was the color brown, while the left was partially hazel, with one section of her iris having a glint of a reddish tone in it. I couldn't help myself at times, doing the same thing as others and staring at it. Many in her circle often regarded her left eye to be the "evil eye". It was like staring into an abyss of malice when confronting her face-to-face. One not knowing if a meeting with Gabriella would be considered a last.

For everything scandalously deadly about her looks, Gabriella was straight business when it came to drugs and a very dangerous person to ever cross. She had a network of hundreds of people working for her in the states and a tumultuous amount of men and women back in Brazil constantly turning the wheels of her ever expanding drug empire.

It was a business she took over with a vengeance the day her husband, Hidalgo Sanchez, was gunned down by federal agents in what was considered one of the biggest drug busts in Columbia's history, she told me while opening up one day. Acting on instructions left by Sanchez, Gabriella had withdrawn whatever emergency money there was and fled the country, laying low for several months. It was at this time Gabriella had pondered leaving the drug world behind her altogether. She had a few million dollars and could have easily started a new life for herself. She sympathized with me when I dealt with those same exact feelings. Telling her one day that I was leaving town. But just like her, it's very hard to let go.

Gabriella explained it as a combination of greed and the thrill associated with drugs and making money that fueled her. She absolutely loved it. It was also the status. Why not? Gabriella had always embraced the limelight, even as a little child.

She told me her life's story once. How she was born in the capital city of Fortaleza, Ceara, Brazil. Daughter to a smart and wealthy businessman by the name of Fausto Braga who made a huge name for himself in the textile industry. He would later reap greater rewards in life by investing in a small energy corporation at the time by the name of Petrobas. Little did Fausto know, Petrobas would grow into a behemoth of a company becoming one of the largest in Brazil and eighth biggest in the world.

As the family fortunes grew, so did the spoiled offerings to his only child.

Gabriella was thrust into a world of money, the best clothes and jewelry, schools, cars, and houses.

She had even become a popular face of the Petrobas company, appearing in several commercials that aired in the seventies, promoting the future of Petrobas and what it meant to the environment.

At the age of twenty-two, Gabriella had been enrolled in the prestigious Pontificia Universidad Catholica de Sao Paulo, studying for a degree in psychology. And as her studious side remained focused with the books, she said it was that spoiled rich kid syndrome that had her frequenting the night club scene mixed with booze and all kinds of drugs.

It is here where she would meet her future husband, Colombian native, Hidalgo Sanchez. Based out in his homeland, Sanchez started out as a basic drug runner slowly climbing up the ladder through the years. With each profit he netted, it was stashed away until he was able to purchase a bulk of his own stuff, slowly hitting the streets and trying to make a name for himself. Once in Brazil, Sanchez had already reached that elite plateau of drug stardom, a well-established figure who was making around two million dollars a year.

He would make his frequent stops in Brazil, checking in on various facilities where his cocaine was converted and refined. It was the intricate details of drug smuggling taught to Sanchez by the best. He had learned about Brazil being the only South American country where ether and acetone, two main ingredients needed to turn coca base into cocaine, were manufactured in industrial quantities. Sanchez was also made privy to the poorly patrolled borders of Bolivia and Brazil, making it easy for runners to transship their bundles of pure cocaine through the Sao Paulo and Rio de Janeiro airports without incident or hassle. It was a money maker with a sky's-the-limit potential to yield more and more money. And that's what Sanchez was striving for.

As time passed, Gabriella and Sanchez were fast becoming an item. And she instantly saw a difference in the way people around her would act. Gabriella always knew that her wealthy background gained her popularity wherever she went, but it was the respect that was being shown to her which she really focused on. It was the instant service given to them whenever they walked into a club or restaurant. Upon entering, it was the whispering and murmuring being done by people as they walked passed them. Police officers, politicians, lawyers, and athletes, all flocking around them just wanting to mix and mingle and rub elbows.

Gabriella was fascinated by this, and she continued to eat it all up.

She had even seen the drug business rear its ugly side, the painful consequences inflicted on a person who owed money, a rival dealer caught off guards, or someone that ratted on Sanchez and his people.

Gabriella watched it all and grew more and more emotionless as time went on. She understood the concept of this kind of business and how it worked. She wouldn't even flinch anymore when a gun went off, nor did she look away after some of the more severe tactics were used on some individuals. In fact, it was kind of exciting to her, she said.

In just short of a year, Gabriella had dropped her studies, gotten married, got into a huge argument with her parents that resulted in not speaking with them for several years, and even moving to Columbia.

She spent the next several years learning about the

business, day-to-day operations, visiting factories,

keeping books and numbers. She was forever present

at meetings her husband was engaged in. She knew

all his contacts, buyers and extra suppliers, and who

his enemies were. She made sure she knew

everything and anything she needed to know about

the drug world she inhabited.

And then she took control of it, all by herself.

••••••••••

The very first meeting between Rolando and

Gabriella had been set up by Kiko "El Machuco"

Hernandez. A very short gentleman with a stocky

build. He had known Rolando for quite some time

and was considered his right hand man who had a knack for meeting people and making new connects. According to Rolando, the meeting this time, was with a new a new supplier, some big-time woman by the name of Gabriella, who another person had introduced Kiko to at a function one night.

Kiko had supposedly swiped at his oily bang, brushing it to one side as he looked up at the elevator floor panel. The light was on floor twelve and going up. Meanwhile, Rolando stood next to him, he told me once, with his head down and eyes closed.

"Hey, what are you doing man, praying?" Kiko asked.

"Just resting my eyes," Rolando said he answered him.

"Listen Rolando, everything is cool okay. This lady is good business. Out of everyone we are involved with, she's the Real Deal McNeal. Top shit. You'll see. I'm telling you," Kiko told him.

"Vamor a ver, Kiko. Let's see if you're right bro," Rolando answered.

Rolando said he was a tad nervous, although he was trying his best not to show it. He knew that this was one of the bigger meetings he was about to step into. And it was all because of this out-of-nowhere woman by the name of Gabriella Braga and her sudden stature.

He'd already heard a ton of things about this woman other than Kiko's mouth. Some of it was good, while other stuff was quite unpleasant. The bad parts all having to do with various people befalling some kind of serious mal because they figured themselves, smarter, tougher or stronger than Gabriella.

At this point though, Rolando had no choice. He had to meet this woman people were raving about. It was a huge business opportunity, perhaps expanding his sales overseas. And lastly, Rolando was itching to meet the woman who had snatched up the six bricks of cocaine that Chester brought to him four months ago. Gabriella paid top dollar he said, shelling out fifteen thousand dollars per brick for a total of ninety thousand dollars cash with no questions asked.

Rolando said he looked up at the floor panel. The elevator had finally stopped on the penthouse floor, thirty seven floors up from ground level. A long way to have to go down if something were to go wrong. He and Kiko then exited the elevator and turned right. They headed towards the only apartment on

this penthouse floor, all belonging to Gabriella Braga.

"You ready?" Kiko asked.

Rolando said he nodded his head as Kiko raised

his hand and rang the doorbell. Within seconds, a

brooding, jacked-up gentleman in a tight grey colored

suit opened the door.

"You Kiko and Rolando?" the man spoke in a deep

voice.

"Si hermanito, what's up, brother?" Kiko replied.

The man just continued to stare at them until a

voice in the background was heard to allow Kiko and

Rolando to enter. With that said, the huge

bodybuilder man stepped aside, nodding his head for

the two men to enter the apartment. Rolando, often

talkative when drunk, told me how Kiko walked in

first followed by him. Rolando tried scanning his

surroundings without looking too suspicious. He said

he was still consumed with everything he saw

anyway.

A triangular shaped glass table upon entering. A

black colored leather sofa that took up a lot of space.

The beige colored area rug and another table in the

middle of the room. There were various exotic

paintings hanging throughout. A pool table towards a

far off corner of the apartment where two gentlemen

were engaged in a game for money, evident by the

stack of bills near one of the corner pockets.

There was a bar in another corner of the room, a

marble counter with three stools, one of them being

occupied by a gentleman in a suit with wiry framed

glasses on. He seemed to be drinking a martini, a

marble notebook next to the glass. A darker colored

gentleman stood behind the bar pouring himself a

drink—Bacardi, on the rocks. His name was Gilberto
Andrade, a big-shot who knew someone that Kiko
knew and so on and so on.

"Gilberto, que pasa mi amigo?" Kiko yelled out,
asking his friend what was up.

"Aqui, aqui. How are you? Gilberto answered him,
motioning for him to come here.

Gilberto now walked out from around the bar with
his drink and shook Kiko's hand.

"Gil, this here is my friend and the man I've been
talking to you about, Rolando Pintero," Kiko said.

Gilberto walked over to Rolando as the two
gentlemen also shook hands. Rolando always said
how he never liked Gilberto. I didn't blame him.

"Where you from, Boricua?" Gilberto had said to
him, implying he was Puerto Rican.

"No. I was born in Cuba," Rolando said he answered.

"Get out man? We have in here a Cuban native, a revolutionary like Che Guevara. I'm sorry I can't make you a mojito, heh," Gilberto was sort of being a dickhead as he spoke.

"Guevara was born in Argentina, Gilbert," Jamison now calmly spoke as he took a light sip of his martini.

I often found it amusing how Jamison and Gilberto interacted with each other. Rolando said he could sense something between the two of them the night he met them. He said Gilberto quickly turned towards Jamison and shot him a serious look after his remark. He then looked back at Rolando and Kiko.

"Anyway, can I get you two something to drink in the meantime? We have all kinds of liquors, some

Bacardi, Vodka maybe, what are you having?"
Gilberto asked them.

"I'll take the same thing you're having, that's fine
with me," Rolando said.

"Y tu Kik?" Gilberto had looked over at Kiko and
asked.

"Lo mismo," Kiko replied he would also have the
same.

"Fine, fine. Go ahead and have a seat my friends,
Gabriella will be out in a few minutes," he said
Gilberto told them as they finally sat down
continuing to look around the apartment, impressed.

Meanwhile, Gilberto had walked back behind the
bar and reached for two glasses and began making
two more drinks. "So Rolando, Kiko tells me you're
the man to see if we need some things out in the

Bronx, is that true?" Gilberto now said as he poured some Bacardi into the glasses.

"Yes, I guess we're doing okay," Rolando supposedly answered him.

"What do you have?" Gilberto asked.

"What are you looking for?" Rolando countered with a question of his own, he told me.

"Me personally, I prefer it to snow all year round. I heard you have some good stuff," Gilberto then said.

"Then you may have heard wrong," Rolando replied.

Rolando knew he was being tested in some ways by Gilberto. He said how he looked off to the side, how he could see Jamison nonchalantly raising his martini to take another sip.

"Why don't you stop it Gilbert?" he said Jamison blurted out.

At this point, Gilberto had leaned in towards Jamison and whispered something to the effect of, "And why don't you just mind your fucking business?"

Suddenly, Gabriella had walked into the room.

"While you're there, why don't you make me a drink as well?" Gabriella said looking in Gilberto's direction.

Rolando described Gabriella as everything being true about her looks and probably better even in person. Her long black hair was straightened. She wore this colorful designer blouse along with a pair of black pants and some red heels. He said both he and Kiko immediately stood up as she approached them and shook hands with them.

"Please, please. Let us sit down," Gabriella said to them as they all sat while Gilberto walked over with a tray of drinks and placed it on the marble table in front of them.

At this moment, Rolando would get a glimpse of how defiant Gabriella was when she instructed Gilberto to basically take a walk with everyone else in the room other than Jamison.

"And what about Jamison?" Gilberto had asked her.

"He stays," Gabriella replied.

"But, I thought you wanted me..." Gilberto tried speaking again.

"Esta bien. You can go now!" Gabriella would ultimately snap back, waving him off with an 'it's fine'.

Rolando retold the story about how Gilberto had slowly walked away grumbling to himself as he turned around. He began to whistle over at the men playing pool who immediately put their cues down and followed after him without saying a word. It was Gabriella keeping a watchful eye on the four gentlemen until they had finally exited.

This next part, I fully believed Gabriella when she told me her side of the story and how she would eventually persuade Rolando to work for her.

"I apologize for Gilberto. He can be a little overbearing at times," Gabriella explained.

"And rude," Jamison would add.

"Yes, and rude. Kiko, Rolando. I want to introduce you to my personal advisor, Jamison," Gabriella said.

"Mr. Jamison. How are you?" Kiko said as looked over at the bar.

"Just Jamison," Jamison quickly answered.

"He's very adamant about that. I suggest you take heed of his request, gentlemen. Now tell me, Kiko says you have some good quality stuff. Although I'll be honest with you. I'm not really into the greens. Not profitable enough for me. What I am interested in, is the heroin," Gabriella told them.

"You seem to have the coca in good motion, making some good money, why heroin?" Rolando questioned her.

"Mister Pintero, is that a problem?" Gabriella now asked.

"No, not at all. And I apologize if it came off that way. I just, I hear good things about you, pretty big things. I just don't think we're on your level. I mean, why speak with us?" Rolando would say.

"Two things. I believe in this business one should never limit themselves. I stay away from the marijuana because I feel the overall profit is obtainable through deals with a younger market. And the last thing I want is some young punk thinking he's bigger than the world, meeting with him while he sits across from me, perhaps some gold in his mouth, a few chains around his neck, and he can't even differentiate between a collector's edition Penfolds Grange bottle of Cabernet and the cheap shit he buys for his girlfriend at the local liquor store. I want a product that has people coming back for more and more, several times if possible in just one day. The coca does that. Crack is getting bigger and bigger.

And the heroin? Well, that's been around for years." Gabriella said to both men.

"Those are some serious long term plans. I've never met someone who thrives on depravity more than you," Rolando would say.

"The most depraved type of human being, is the man without purpose. Or in this case, woman. Isn't that correct Gabriella," Jamison chimed in.

"That's correct, Jamison. And my purpose in life, is to corner the market, whatever market on whatever product I'm going to sell, and make the most money I can." Gabriella said, supposedly with a devilish smile for good measure.

"I guess I can respect that. So Gabriella tell us, what is the other thing you speak about?" Rolando asked as he had taken a sip from his drink.

Gabriella later told me how she looked at Rolando square in the eyes, her smile disappearing.

"With that Rolando, I'll cut straight through the bullshit. Are you familiar with a man by the name of Martine Rosa?" Gabriella asked him.

"No. I can't say that I am," Rolando answered while shaking his head.

"It was back in October that mister Rosa had some product of his that was stolen in some big bust that went horribly wrong out in Brooklyn. It was that same cocaine that I purchased from your friend Kiko here. You do know what cocaine I'm talking about, right? Six bricks of pure uncut product. Very decent quality I must admit, and that is a huge compliment coming from me," Gabriella would say in her usual monotone voice.

She told me how it seemed as if Rolando wanted to look away but just didn't. He squinted his eyes, probably burning him as he desperately remained focused on her. This was one of those times where a person had to show what they were made of, even though the meeting may have taken a turn for the worst. Gabriella had taught me this. She told me how I would eventually have my share of those exact moments. She said Rolando then spoke with a little nervousness in his voice.

"I was doing someone a favor and trying to get rid of it, that's all. I had no personal ties to this product being stolen," Rolando said.

"Your brother-in-law, Chester Cepeda, correct?" Gabriella countered.

"Yes. That is correct," Rolando answered.

"Does he know about it?" She asked him.

"I would think he does," Rolando replied.

Gabriella's side of the story goes that she stood up and walked over to the counter with her drink in hand.

"Tell me Rolando, are you familiar with a man by the name of Marlon. Marlon Nathaniel White?" Gabriella continued asking questions.

"Yes. He was with Chester the day they brought me the bricks," Rolando said to her.

"Well, I'll bet you these two men weren't really being up front with you when they showed you what they had," she said.

"Chester told me it was lifted off some punks, new jacks or something. No one important," Rolando spoke again.

"Not quite, Mister Pintero. They were also involved with a third person, Jermaine Grant, another local punk who was shot and killed the night of the bust. That my friend, is your main concern right now," Gabriella said she told him.

"My concern? What do you mean? I don't understand what is going on here," Rolando replied.

Gabriella described Rolando as seeming lost and confused as Jamison stood up from his seat and walked over to him and Kiko.

"Mr. Pintero, it's a shame that you are oblivious to the possible shit storm about to surround you," Jamison said chuckling.

"A storm of which I may just be your only umbrella. The why's and how's of them acquiring this product are insignificant at this moment. I'll tell you what is. Apparently, Marlon remained in contact with Jermaine's girlfriend, he even sent her some money, a gift of sorts for her loss. Afterwards, a drug gang out in Brooklyn known as NLT had put pressure on her, threatening her life and the life of her daughter for Marlon's whereabouts. She panicked and went to the police, but there in police custody, she was forced to work with them for the same information the gang was looking for. They patrolled her apartment, kept tabs on her, they took pictures, and, they tapped her phone lines. What more do you want? Now, I hear there are some phone records in the middle of this investigation that mention your name, multiple times," Gabriella had broken it down to Rolando and Kiko.

"What!?! I... I don't know about all of this. This is crazy. I have nothing to do with any of this," Rolando now seemed upset as he pleaded.

"When was the last time you saw Marlon?" she asked him.

"The only time I met him. That first day I met him in my apartment," Rolando replied.

"Yes. Seems Marlon has gone into hiding once he collected his share of the cash, but he has left another mess. This investigation has potential to reach many different levels, DEA, Federal. Apart from drug dealing, there is also murder charges. The fact that your name is floating around in this, doesn't bode well for your business nor for your health. Your name is the only one out there right now apart from Marlon's, and, word is that the Rosa family has also gotten a hold of this information. And nothing would be better than to find the people involved in taking and getting rid of his product. Do you understand where I'm going with this?" She would explain to Rolando.

Rolando bowed his head into his knees. Perhaps all the information he was trying to process had been hitting him like a whirlwind from hell. The few sips of his Bacardi must have left a bitter taste in his mouth as this bombshell had been thrown right into his lap. I could imagine Rolando being pissed off at that moment. Thinking about how he should take a bat to Chester's head or something and beat him so bloody, to a pulp, no identification would have been made other than forensic dental anatomy. Probably said to himself, *Fuck what Mildred might think!*

Rolando supposedly looked up. He first looked at Kiko, probably marveled that through all of this, Kiko hadn't said a damn word. He then looked over at Gabriella and Jamison.

"How do you know all of this?" He asked them.

"I am not in the position I am in today without the help of many people, some of which happen to be on the opposite sides of the spectrum. With that said, I am willing to help you," Gabriella then answered him.

"How?" Rolando now asked.

"Well, right now you're just a name to detectives and the Rosa family. The key component in all of this is Mister White. A very damaged and unsocial miscreant snake who doesn't know how to keep his mouth shut. For that he has many enemies I'm told. The fact that he has also acted as an informant for police means, whomever gets to him first, he will definitely sing," Gabriella explained.

"So what do you suggest I should do?" Rolando asked deflated.

"I believe you may need to have a serious word with Chester and find out what he knows, if he knows anything about where Marlon is hiding out. This way we can ensure that this entire mess is handled properly," Gabriella told him.

"Why are you so concerned with Marlon, or me for that matter?" Rolando would then ask.

"You and your partner can walk out that front door right now and do whatever you like. You'll deal with whatever comes your way however you can and see fit. Like I said, the law will continue to do their jobs, meaning, it's a matter of time before they commence some kind of full blown investigation, swarming the streets of the Bronx for Rolando Pintero. If they haven't already. Now, while I cannot wholly make you untouchable to the authorities, I can ease the pressure somewhat. Perhaps my assistant

Jamison here can have a word with Mister Grant's girlfriend. Or if he likes, make her disappear. The real issue here is Martine Rosa. I can use you to get to him. Let's call it, something I need to do for my own personal reasons. If you decide yes, you can be rest assured that in the process, I can also make you a very rich man," Gabriella said she spoke to Rolando with a serious tone.

"You have all this access to information, money, and whatever else you need. Why not get to Rosa some other way?" Rolando continued asking questions.

"The fact that I ended up purchasing a shitload of mister Rosa's coca was like a Godsend. A gift that happened to come my way. But, I have bigger plans for Rosa and I can use you to get closer to him than I ever possibly imagined. I'm sure that an intelligent man like yourself surely knows that in this business,

no amount of money in the world can buy one

thing—and that is trust," she told him.

"That has to be earned." Rolando was said to have

answered intelligently.

"Precisely. So it basically comes down to you. Your

move, Mister Pintero," Gabriella then said.

She said Rolando thought about the offer being

given to him. How he looked already defeated in

many ways. Probably felt as if his entire funds

already vested and the people he had working for

him were about to be stripped. Something that

Gabriella could have done in a heartbeat if she

wanted. She could see him reflect on how Rolando

was about to become a bitch working for a bitch. A

very meticulous and calculated one at that. Rolando

then reached out to her with his hand. They both shook on it.

Despite their teaming up of sorts, Gabriella told me how she never put too much trust in anyone. That part of her tactics and way of business never changed at all. Her instincts about Rolando would obviously be validated when he finally snapped, I guess, and fled town.

It was funny to me. I spent a lot of time always gathering information, hearing stories from different people, but in the end, I still always had to add my own assumptions. Gabriella could be quite difficult to deal with at times. And so was Rolando. I basically don't really know who was to blame for everything getting out of hand? All I do know is that I would eventually be thrust right in the middle of all the bullshit one day.

Chapter 12

"One by One, They All Fall Down"

[TUESDAY, MAY 15, 1990

10:45 P.M.]

911 Phone Operator: "9-1-1, what is your emergency?"

Antonio Pintero: *(crying)* "I need an ambulance. My mother's not breathing, she's not moving."

911 Phone Operator: "Your mother?"

Antonio Pintero: "Yes, my mother."

911 Phone Operator: "Sir, what is your name?"

Antonio Pintero: "Antonio Pintero. Please I can't...*(Inaudible)*"

911 Phone Operator: "Can you spell that for me?"

Antonio Pintero: "A-N-T-O-N-I-O"

911 Phone Operator: "Antonio, correct?"

Antonio Pintero: "Yes!"

911 Phone Operator: "Okay, Antonio, how old are you?"

Antonio Pintero: "My mother… (Inaudible… It's not working."

911 Phone Operator: "What's not working, Antonio?"

Antonio Pintero: "I'm trying to do CPR"

911 Phone Operator: "You know how to perform CPR?"

Antonio Pintero: "Yes."

911 Phone Operator: "Antonio, can you tell me how old you are?"

Antonio Pintero: "I'm fourteen. Please send an ambulance. She's not moving, please. I can't… (Inaudible)… "

911 Phone Operator: "You're fourteen? Is this correct?"

Antonio Pintero: "Yes, fourteen! 1-4!"

911 Phone Operator: "Okay, Antonio, baby. Listen to me. I need you to speak slowly and give me your address, okay?"

Antonio Pintero: "Yes. It's 3439 Knox Place. Apartment 6F."

911 Phone Operator: "That's 3-4-3-9 Knox. K-N-O-X Place? Is that correct?"

Antonio Pintero: "Yes, yes, yes, yes!"

911 Phone Operator: "And you said apartment 6 F or S?"

Antonio Pintero: "F as in FRANK."

911 Phone Operator: "Okay, that's 3439 Knox Place, apartment 6F as in Frank. Now baby, is there anyone else in the apartment with you?"

Antonio Pintero: No, just me. There's blood on my hands now."

911 Phone Operator: "What? Did you say blood?"

Antonio Pintero: "There's… *(Inaudible)…* "

911 Phone Operator: "Antonio, are you there sweetheart? Talk to me."

Antonio Pintero: "Yes, I'm here."

911 Phone Operator: "You said there is blood?"

Antonio Pintero: "It's on my hands now."

911 Phone Operator: "From where? Antonio?"

Antonio Pintero: "My hands! My fucking hands! I was trying to lift her up and put her on the bed… *(Inaudible)…*"

911 Phone Operator: "The blood Antonio, is that from your mother?"

Antonio Pintero: "It's coming from her head, I think."

911 Phone Operator: "Okay listen to me, baby. Did your mother fall? Did she bang her head, is that the reason for the blood?"

Antonio Pintero: "I don't know, maybe."

911 Phone Operator: "Antonio, I want you to listen to me, okay? I have dispatched an ambulance to this address already. But, I need you to remain calm. If you mother hit her head, you do not want to attempt to move her. Do you hear me?"

(MUFFLED NOISES)

911 Phone Operator: "Hello? Antonio are you still there?"

Antonio Pintero: "Yes. She's not fucking moving!"

(REPEATED BANGING)

Antonio Pintero: *(Uncontrollable crying)* "Fuck! I have blood all over me!"

···········

I'd been out the night my mother died. It was business as usual for me. Right after school I had gone over to Duckie's crib and dropped off my book bag. There we went over what bags of weed we both had left, bundled with Taz and Jose's remaining ones; afterwards, we bounced to work. I remember meeting up with Rolando around six in the evening. I kept harassing him about needing more weed. The last few months had been pretty good and I was going through about a pound every ten days it seemed.

Between the Foo Crew putting in their work, and Rosemary's brother, things were looking good.

The only problem at that time was the constant waiting I had to do in order to get my product from Rolando. I had noticed he didn't really care too much about the marijuana like he once did. He'd been hanging out an awful lot with his boy Kiko, Chester, and some new guys who I didn't care much about, especially this smug acting son of a bitch by the name of Gilberto.

Word on the streets was this new woman partner of his was the big shit. I had met her a few times. I admit, she was bad as hell. I know my moms hated her. She couldn't get the crazy notion out of her head that Rolando may have been piping down Gabriella. I know Rolando wished it to be true though. I even caught myself fantasizing about Gabriella. She was the one that pushed Rolando to keep supplying me with the weed. She'd seen what my business was like and respected my hustle for a kid.

I remember meeting up with Rosemary about eight. We hung out in the stairwell of her apartment building. Her mother didn't like me much so we often had to do all our hanging out together outside in the streets. Rosemary and I were getting closer. We were up to doing certain things but not quite having had sex all the way yet. I stayed with her for about an hour and left. I also had a hickie on my neck courtesy of Rosemary who often liked to mark me out of her own jealous thinking. She figured any bitch that saw the love bruise would get the hint I belonged to someone. Like that really stopped the hood rats?

I ended up back at Duckie's crib around nine-thirty. I had to pick up my stuff plus collect some money that Jose had dropped off. Duck and I talked for a few, while we smoked like four cigarettes each. I couldn't help it. I saw all my friends around me smoking, the people that bought off of us smoking, Rolando, and my mother, so it was just another habit I blamed on my surroundings.

I finally got to my building about ten thirty. I put the keys in the door and opened it. The hall light was on plus the light in the kitchen. My mother always wanted some kind of light in the apartment. She said it helped in keeping the roaches hidden. I often went straight to my room, dropped my book bag and headed into the bathroom. I then went straight into my mother's room and that's when I found her.

My mother was in a stained and ragged nightgown, on the floor near her bed. Autopsy report said my mother had suffered a seizure at one point while on her way back from the bathroom or something. She'd fallen back and hit her head on the corner of the nightstand. The progression of AIDS in her system had dropped her CD4-T cells so low, my mother had developed something called PML. This was short for Progressive Multifocal Leukoencephalopathy. It was described as a viral disease which had progressively been damaging the white matter in her brain. It was also the cause of her sometimes incoherent, slurred speech, and clumsiness when she attempted to walk around the apartment.

Nobody knew. No doctors, Rolando, no one. I remember panicking. I desperately tried performing CPR on her until I finally grabbed the phone and dialed 911. While holding the phone to my ear and grabbing on to my mother, I also tried lifting her, trying to put her back on the bed. That's when I freaked out even more. The crusted up wound on the back of her head must have opened allowing the cut to bleed some more. It was getting all over my hands. While I was dealing with the emotional angst of my moms on the floor not moving, the possibility of her being dead at that moment—I also started panicking because her tainted blood was now getting on me as well.

....

There weren't too many people that attended my mother's wake. It was sad actually. Apart from the low turn-out, the only innocent people there were my grandmother and my brother Miguel. Everyone else was either some kind of felon, career criminal, drug dealer, or addict. My friends and I were no better. Rolando was there, Kiko, Chester, a few cousins that crawled out of the wood works who I didn't know. That guy Gilberto was there, Gabriella even passed through, and some people from the neighborhood who knew my mother and wanted to pay their respects.

Towards the end of the night, a little frail old black woman entered the funeral parlor being pushed in a wheelchair by a nurse's aide. They rolled right passed everyone and headed straight for the casket. The woman strained a bit but managed to get up from her chair and stood in front of my mother's body just staring at her. I remember my grandmother getting up from her seat and walking over to this old woman.

They exchanged a few words and then embraced each other with the sincerest and strongest of hugs I had ever seen. For a quick second, I kind of felt jealous. I don't think my grandmother had ever hugged me as strong as she did this woman. I would later find out this older woman was Adina Roberts. My grandmother and she had found a way to regain contact with each other through a mutual friend.

Adina had been living in Florida and flew in for the funeral upon hearing the news of my mother's death. I was introduced to Adina, but very briefly. My grandmother knew what I did and usually kept any introductions to a minimum for fear of being humiliated I guess. It was cool with me though. I had fully accepted many things in my life up to that point and being the apple of someone's eye? — I knew I was definitely not. In fact, once my mother died, I fully believe is when I actually got worse. I know the relationship with me and my mother was oftentimes a strained one. But I cared for her, I really did. When Mildred died. My heart got colder.

•••••••••

Several months had gone by since my mother had passed away. Rolando and I remained living in the apartment although there were many times I would go a long stretch without seeing him. In order to fill the void of having some kind of company, I would let my friends stay with me whenever they liked. We separated our product, weighed and bagged it. We smoked, drank, and just hung out. Even Rosemary was stopping by on a regular basis. The two of us would order food and watch movies. We'd roll an occasional blunt here and there and smoke until we were both red-eyed and high. We'd also eventually take our relationship to the next level by finally going all the way.

It was a hot August day; the temperature outside had reached about 94 degrees and the apartment was beginning to swelter. This was due to the only AC in the apartment being busted and neither Rolando or myself ever made a move to purchase a new one. Rosemary had stopped by the apartment around ten in the morning. I'd given her a set of keys and told her she could use them whenever she liked. This day, she had been kind enough to bring me some breakfast, the Dominican special, consisting of scrambled eggs, fried sausage, fried white cheese and some Mangu, pureed green banana with red onions.

I'd spoken to her earlier and told her that I might be in the shower when she arrived. Sure enough, I could faintly hear the front door slam as she entered the apartment.

Rosemary said when we would reminisce later that she headed straight to the kitchen and placed the paper bag down on the table. She also said how she could hear me attempt to rap while I bathed, which made her smile and then giggle.

I remember the apartment was hot. It seemed like every window throughout the place was opened and yet there was no hint of any cool air blowing in through any of them. Rosemary said how she even opened the refrigerator and reached for a can of soda. How the can was nice and cold and how she pressed it against her forehead to cool down some.

Afterwards, Rosemary walked towards the bathroom
door and knocked on it.

"Yoo-hoo I'm home, sweetie," she said jokingly.

"Real funny. I'll be out in a few minutes, I'm
almost finished," I answered her.

"I brought you some food," Rosemary told me.

"Okay. I'll be right out I said!" Screaming less now.

"Fine. With your nasty attitude!" I could hear her
scream back at me.

Rosemary headed into the bedroom as she sat on
the bed and glanced over at the television, she said.
She'd opened the soda and took a swig and then left it
on the window sill as she checked the fan. I know the
thing had been dialed on the highest setting and yet it
felt like nothing was blowing out. She said she placed

her face in front of the fan just to feel some kind of air

blowing.

Rosemary had apparently turned around and

leaned her head back. She let the wind blow through

her hair as she continued struggling to cool down.

She kicked off her sandals as she closed her eyes. She

could feel a slight breeze as it whispered on the nape

of her neck, she smiled she told me. Rosemary said

how she was starting to feel weird. Something was

coming over her, she was feeling giddy all of a

sudden. She said she felt like unbuttoning her khaki

colored shorts and pulling down the zipper. Which

she did. She continued to lay there with her eyes

closed.

That's how I found her, when I walked into the

bedroom. I was shirtless with just the towel wrapped

around my waist. I immediately saw Rosemary on the

bed, her painted toes dangling off the edge. I saw her pants semi-opened. As I got closer, I could clearly see the form of her erect nipples through her black tube top. This was starting to excite me.

"Rosemary. What are you doing?" I said to her.

She opened her eyes and looked at me. She clearly saw my erection starting to come alive through the wrapped towel. She then looked up at me.

"Waiting for you. Come over here, Antonio," she whispered to me in a very low and sexy type voice.

Without hesitation, I walked over to the bed and got on top of Rosemary as we immediately began to kiss. It was definitely starting to get hot and heavy, I could feel my erection getting harder by the passing second. So bad that it was starting to hurt even. I now slid my hand underneath her shirt and started squeezing her breasts. They were firm as I gently used my finger and lightly made a circular motion around her right nipple. I then proceeded to slide my hand back out and down her stomach and into her panties. I used the same middle finger and quickly stuck it inside her as we continued kissing. Rosemary was extra wet it felt and all of this just made me want her even more.

Rosemary moaned as she leaned in and started to kiss me on my neck. I closed my eyes, her sucking on my neck gave me chills. At this precise moment, I wasn't thinking about anything else but to make love to her, not even caring whether or not she was marking my neck with an extra purple colored hickey. I was getting more and more vulnerable as she rolled her tongue around and then bit on my neck, pulling on the skin.

That was it. I couldn't help it anymore. I pulled away and excitedly pulled down her pants along with her panties. I then ripped off the towel and pulled Rosemary closer towards me. We didn't really think about what we were going to do, we didn't talk about it. It was just one of those spur of the moment things, a spontaneous act our bodies couldn't hold off any longer. It was happening right there and then.

I slipped my cock inside her. No words, no condom. And Rosemary just let me.

··········

I always envisioned certain scenes in my head whenever Jamison told me stories. One of them had to do with a woman by the name of Shawnee Watkins who he followed to a laundry place one late night.

She was the supposed girlfriend of some guy that was involved with my uncle's famous drug heist that went down in Brooklyn. He was eventually shot and killed. This woman on the other hand, became some kind of cheap and sad collateral damage in Gabriella's bigger plans in order to coax Rolando into helping her with Rosa. By eliminating one person, Rolando was to see that Gabriella was a person of her word and seriously a dangerous woman.

Jamison told me how he observed the woman through the window of the laundromat while he sat in his car. Shawnee Watkins had let out a low yawn as she slowly folded the last item of her laundry. It was a burgundy colored T-shirt that appeared to be imprinted with a Babar decal on it. The shirt must have belonged to her five-year-old daughter ,Soriyah, who was at home with her grandmother at the time.

Jamison was definitely thorough with his targets whenever sent out on his little seek and destroy missions.

Shawnee made it a habit of visiting the twenty-four hour laundromat late at night. Probably one of those people that liked the fact it was less crowded during the wee hours and that she was able to eliminate a chore without having to drag her daughter with her. Jamison explained how Shawnee did this once a week.

Shawnee supposedly placed the item in a yellow colored laundry bag and then placed the bag into her black and beat up looking grocery cart. The damn thing was on its last legs. It was evident when the right amount of weight was put inside. The left wheel immediately started to creak and wobble as she pushed it past the laundry attendant, Jamison said.

It was a little past one in the morning as Shawnee pushed her cart into the parking lot. The temperature out was a mild and pleasant 62 degrees as she unzipped her jacket.

The parking lot appeared crowded but only because some of the area locals would leave their cars in the lot overnight. Shawnee was even culpable of the same exact thing on occasions, Jamison said. He'd only been following her for several weeks he added. It was her being lazy and not wanting to wake up so early in the morning to move her car from one side of the block to the other probably; yet another opinion offered by Jamison. As Shawnee neared her vehicle, she raised her keys in the air and pressed the alarm button. Just one beep was heard and the sound of a click and her car doors were instantly unlocked.

Shawnee pushed her cart to the back of the vehicle and opened the trunk. She proceeded to fight with her yellow laundry bag, wriggling and prying it out from the cart. She would finally heave the bag and dump it into the back of the car, folding on her fragile cart next and throwing laundry on top. The whole process of washing, drying, folding, pushing and lifting had broken a sweat as she used the back of her hand to wipe it off. All the while, Jamison had been in his car two spots away trying to get the thing started. Yet, another ploy of his to make his reason for being in the lot all the more believable.

Shawnee closed her trunk and was about to head for the driver's side when in the corner of her eye she must have noticed a white gentleman approaching her.

"Excuse me, excuse me, young lady," Jamison said he called out to her.

"Yes?" She responded.

"I'm sorry to bother you. Would you be able to help me? My car isn't starting and I was wondering if you might be able to tell me of the nearest gas station around here?" Jamison was to have said to her.

"You gonna have to walk over to Linden. There's a gas station across the street from the diner. I know a bunch of cab service guys be there at this time, maybe one of them can help you," she supposedly said. Jamison was even on point with her improper diction when telling the story.

"You're an angel. Thank you very much. The last thing I want to do is get stuck in this neighborhood with some of these people," he told me he answered her. He said he knew exactly well his remark would get a reaction, which it did.

"What!?!? What the fuck did you just say?" Shawnee barked as she continued to look at the weird looking man who had now walked away.

What both Gabriella and Jamison knew how to do—they really knew how to mind fuck people. That's how good they were. Shawnee was pissed off at that point. She couldn't help but keep thinking about the nasty remark this weird white guy with glasses and leather gloves on had just said to her perhaps. Jamison retold it that when he continued walking away, he could still hear her huffing and puffing about his words.

She'd opened her car door and got inside the car. Must have made some remark of her own perhaps, "Fucking racist motherfucker!" Shawnee must have put the keys into the ignition, still thinking about the white gentleman with glasses on and his idiotic comment. It was probably hot inside the car. She'd been sweating before. Probably more so now having worked herself up from being pissed off.

She must have then turned her keys halfway, enough to power the car's windows as she zipped the front ones down. Jamison said her radio came on. The song playing quickly brought a smile to her face as she began to bop her head. Shawnee then saw Jamison again. After retrieving something from his car he had walked past the front of her car and headed towards the exit. She couldn't help but lean her head out the window.

"You stupid ass fuck. I hope you get robbed. Dumbass wearing gloves and it's hot outside," she yelled at him.

In Jamison's cynical thought process, he would always make references to what last thought people would come across right before something bad happened to them? In Shawnee's case, what was she thinking of when she next turned the keys in the ignition all the way? The motor sparked and turned on.

And then....

Jamison told me how the car exploded with such ferocity that a few of the laundromat's front windows shattered into pieces. A giant fire ball had burst upwards lighting up the Brooklyn sky. In a flash, a crowd of people started to run outside from their buildings, the corner deli, and the laundromat. All they could see was the burnt silhouette of Shawnee's body behind the wheel.

....

Gabriel Rosa drove while his brother Frankie rode shotgun. He would frequently look at a yellow piece of paper in his hand trying to make sense of directions to an address. Meanwhile, their father, Martine, sat in the back seat clutching onto his cane as he intently stared outside through the window.

The three of them had been on the road for an hour and a half now and still no sign of arriving at their destination. All Frankie knew was that apart from long stretches of open roads and seeing trees, about fifteen minutes ago they had driven past a sign welcoming them to Blackwood, New Jersey.

"Conio. This is fucked up. Te lo estoy diciendo—
Somebody's messing with you, pa, I'm telling you,"
Gabriel shouted as he continued driving.

"Sigue! We're already out here. What do you want
me to do, huh?" Martine said angrily.

"Relax, we're almost there," Frankie said.

"How do you know?" Gabriel asked him.

" 'Cuz we just passed some barn on the right. It
says it here on the paper. There should be a huge
white house on your left, a big tree in front of it
coming up," Frankie answered.

True to the directions on the paper, fifty yards
away, all of them could see a white house coming up
on the left side.

"There is nothing out here. What the fuck do these people do for fun, or if they need something from the store?" Gabriel said.

"Yo pa, maybe you should open a bodega out in the middle of west bubble fuck! We could make some money over here," Frankie joked.

His father wasn't smiling as he gave his son a menacing look.

"You going to run the place? Maybe I should leave you here now. Que tu crees? Por dios Frankie, callate la boca. You hear me?" Martine barked as he sarcastically asked Frankie what he thought about that idea, pleading to God for him to just shut his mouth.

Frankie immediately shut up as he scanned over the directions one more time. He then fingered his way down the paper. Red barn thing, check. The white house on the left, already passed it. Just two more miles and they would be coming up on yet another barn, to the right. Frankie then looked up. He could see the place in the distance.

"It's over there. The barn. You see it?" He said.

"That barn on the right?" Gabriel asked his brother.

"Yeah. That's the one," Frankie added.

They'd finally arrived. Gabriel slowed the car down as he turned the steering wheel to the right. They went from highway, onto a narrow dirt path surrounded by trees and underbrush. They could hear the rocks crackling under the tires of the car probably filling some of the treads as they got closer to the barn. Just like Frankie had mentioned, they were out in the boondocks and the barn seemed to be situated right in the middle of nowhere, U.S.A.

The car finally stopped as Frankie got out and stretched his arms. He then walked over and opened the back door, aiding his father out of the vehicle. Gabriel meanwhile, had walked over to the back of the car and opened the trunk. He removed a long white colored bag, the black handle of something inside the bag sticking out.

The three gentlemen looked around. The barn was a decrepit looking thing that was in dire need of work. They could easily see the roof was in bad shape, large areas of shingles missing. A door on the side slightly hanging from its hinge. Broken slats of wood, others chipping and curling from erosion and condensation. As they breathed in, the air was foul, the smell of a dead animal perhaps.

Martine and his two sons inched closer to the entrance of the barn. Despite having a cane, Martine carefully tried keeping his balance on the uneven ground littered with tiny stones and an assortment of animal droppings throughout. The foul smell was getting stronger. It was a distinct odor, not much of a carcass anymore, but that of vile and putrid feces. Human feces.

Frankie got in front of his father as he reached out and removed a wooden two-by-four on the barn's door. He pulled on the handle and the door slowly creaked open. Whatever the smell was, it was definitely emitting from within the barn. The three gentlemen clutched at their mouths attempting to block the smell from entering their nostrils any further. It was dark inside.

"Who is that? Who the fuck is there? Please, let me go, please," a crying and scared voice was heard.

As Frankie opened the door wider, the rays of the sun were enough to shine light inside, and they could finally see what they had been looking for.

A naked black gentleman with a burlap sack over his head. He was sitting on a wooden chair, his hands securely tied at the lower rail in back of him. His ankles were also fastened at each of the chairs front legs. As the Rosa men got closer, the man began to writhe in desperation and fear. Gabriel looked at the man up and down, he could notice the stains of blood on his chest mixed with sweat and old vomit. Crusted up shit and stale urine smeared all over the man's bottom and running down the back legs of the chair, onto the ground.

"Quitale el saco ese," Martine instructed as Gabriel took the order to remove the sack from the man's head.

Gabriel slowly walked up to the chair, a disgusted look on his face as he reached out and slowly removed the sack from the man's head. It was Marlon White.

"Please, don't hurt me anymore. Please. I'm sorry, please, please!" He begged for his life.

Martine walked up to Marlon and just stared at him.

"Nobody, steals from me," he said.

"I'm sorry, Rosa. Please, don't hurt me!" Marlon begged.

"My friend. The pain is just beginning," Martine answered him.

Martine reached for the white bag that Gabriel had and removed what was inside. A long black leather shield that encased a very sharp looking machete. He then removed the blade. Marlon squirmed in his chair as Rosa inched the blade closer to his chest. He then began to scream in agonizing pain as the older gentleman began to stab him repeatedly.